WAVERING WARRIOR

TRENCH RAIDERS BOOK 2

THOMAS WOOD

BOLEYNBENNETT PUBLISHING

Copyright © 2019 by Thomas Wood

All rights reserved.

No part of this book may be reproduced in any form or by any electronic or mechanical means, including information storage and retrieval systems, without written permission from the author, except for the use of brief quotations in a book review.

This book is a work of fiction. Names, characters, places, and incidents either are products of the author's imagination or are used fictitiously. Any resemblance to actual persons, living or dead, events, or locales is entirely coincidental.
Thomas Wood

Visit my website at www.ThomasWoodBooks.com

Printed in the United Kingdom

First Printing: February 2019
by
BoleynBennett Publishing

GRAB ANOTHER BOOK FOR FREE

If you enjoy this book, why not pick up another one, completely free?

'Enemy Held Territory' follows Special Operations Executive Agent, Maurice Dumont as he inspects the defences at the bridges at Ranville and Benouville. Fast paced and exciting, this Second World War thriller is one you won't want to miss!
Details can be found at the back of this book.

1

THE PARTY of six men had snuck into the enemy trench completely undetected, a slight scuffle with one of the sentries the only resistance to their entry so far. By the time he had seen the flying silhouette, it was already half a second too late, a knife protruding from his neck, embedded so far into it, that it looked more like a dislocated bone.

The men, blackened faces and stripped of anything that could make an utterance of noise, moved in a perfect silence, as one body, each one knowing perfectly what their task entailed.

For Private Reg Dornan, this was the first sense of a trench raid that he had ever experienced, the only other time he had been able to glean a look inside an enemy trench was a few weeks previous, when he had been part of an advance that had ultimately faltered.

The Germans' trench was high. Sandbagged walls giving off the impression of a well concealed and well protected dugout. Reg knew full well though, the dugouts were anything but well-concealed; his company's sharpshooters had managed to slot twelve enemy soldiers in the space of two weeks. With only one hundred yards between the two frontline trenches, it was a risky business poking your head above the parapet in this sector.

Reg watched his commanding officer, Captain Arnold, intensely, awaiting the moment when he was called forward for action. Reg had his 1907 pattern rifle bayonet in his right hand, his other gripping tightly onto a Mark V Webley revolver, with six .455 calibre rounds sitting expectantly in the cylinder. The revolver was a more than satisfactory fall back plan if the bayonet failed.

Captain Arnold stood over the body of the deceased sentry, as he started to rummage around nearby looking for anything that might be useful to them; a map, a letter with a giveaway in it, maybe even evidence of an advance. None of this was found on the first body, and so, along with Private Earnshaw, he moved on to the other bodies that were now dotted around the place, heads lolled at various angles and arms flailing in all sorts of directions.

Reg was tasked with watching over the Captain and Earnshaw, as they searched the bay for anything that had the faintest whiff of intelligence. Sergeant Hughes was standing over on the far side of the trench, similarly searching what appeared to be a German officer.

Towering above him, in the dim light offered by the cloudy early springtime night, was Lance Corporal McKay, who was meant to be keeping an eye down the next section of trench, but instead was engrossed in what the Sergeant was doing. Reg tried to catch his eye, to purse his lips and flick his head at him to stay focused, but McKay offered him no such chance.

There was something off with him today, thought Reg suddenly, as he realised that McKay hadn't been his normal self the last few days. He was a good soldier, in fact, he was one of the best that Reg had ever come across, but something had changed within him recently.

His father had been a gamekeeper in Scotland, and Christopher McKay had spent hours on the estate helping and learning the trade. He had come into contact with many members of the British aristocracy, and had even met one or two royals, though he was neither proud of the fact nor complimentary about them.

He was quite short, but he was built like a pillar of concrete, with muscles that seemed to bulge even when he was asleep. It was unusual to see a man of his stature shaking from fear, but that's how Reg found him, while he watched over the Sergeant as he finished his search.

The Sergeant looked up sharply at McKay, with a look that said "Buck your ideas up, son." Accompanied with a slight shove towards the end of the bay, McKay seemed to get the message, hauling his revolver up to hip height and twiddling his bayonet in between his fingers.

As he repositioned himself to the end of the zig-zagging trench, the look on his face told Reg that he knew he had messed up. He knew he had seen the German far too late.

For some reason, the Boche didn't stop to think that there might be more of us around the corner, so instead of popping McKay, then lobbing a spherical shaped grenade round the corner, he lunged at the British soldier in front of him.

McKay staggered for a moment, until the second, expert punch caught him square on the nose, and even in the dim light, Reg could see the blood that sprayed from a gaping wound that had opened up on the bridge.

No one moved for half a second, apart from McKay, who slumped backwards, unconscious, into a pile of sandbags that had been half-prepared and were waiting to be deployed.

The German stopped and stared, as if he had been expecting just the one intruder, but quickly burst into action as he produced a Luger pistol. He began waving it wildly for a moment as if to warn all of the raiders that he wasn't afraid to use it.

He enjoyed about a second of pure confidence, standing in his own trench, glaring at his uninvited guests. After which Sergeant Hughes cannoned into the German, trying to knock him off balance and dispose of him quietly. As they had already done with the four or so other bodies that littered the trench.

No sound seemed to emanate from the dugout, except a few thumps and scrapes as the two bodies smashed into the floor of the trench. Hughes managed to land a perfect punch straight to the man's head, which seemed to have no effect on him, for he soon managed to roll over, until he had Hughes pinned to the ground.

McKay groggily awoke, but was quickly pulled to his senses by the sight of his Sergeant scrabbling around in the dirt with a German. Lifting his revolver up to the German's head, he lined up the shot. It was perfect. He couldn't miss.

That was until, the quiver in his arm began to take hold, flicking the revolver in all manner of directions until he tried to steady himself with his other hand. Something *was* wrong with him; he wasn't going to be able to take the shot.

Reg wondered what was racing through his mind as he stood there. Was it out of fear that he couldn't kill the German? Or was it out of a new-found respect for their enemy that he wouldn't squeeze the trigger, or sink his bayonet into him?

Reg could feel everyone screaming at McKay to kill the German; he was in the best position to do so, and to maintain the quietness that would be preferable for a withdrawal. Reg sensed it most from his Captain, who was now burning so much with fury, that he could tell his skin would be a bright red. That was even under all the dirt and charred cork that they had pasted over their faces before the raid.

Eventually, McKay lowered his revolver, his shoulders sinking forwards in defeat. He was done. He wanted no more part of it.

What had happened to him?

He had been the hardest man of all in the party, the one who had shocked Reg with the fear and reality of what it was like to go over in the middle of the night. He was the one that had all the stories floating around him, the rumours that he would kill even those who had surrendered themselves to him.

And now, here he was, on the verge of tears, unable to kill an enemy soldier, even though he was trying earnestly to butcher his Sergeant.

In a flash, Captain Arnold took the initiative, picking up his solid wood, police style baton and striding over to the tussling bodies, not caring how much noise he made along the gradually rotting duckboards.

He waited for a moment, until the German teed his own head up nicely for him. Arnold instantly took his chance and raised his arm up, high above his head.

Clump.

There was a soft thud as the baton made contact with the German's skull, but there seemed to be a delay before the German registered what had happened and his body slumping over unconscious into the sandbag-walled parapet.

Reg was filled with an overwhelming sense of relief and triumph, which was experienced by all in the trench, not least Sergeant Hughes, who was immediately gasping for breath and recovering from the fracas.

The relief was short lived. As the German's body continued to fall to the ground, his pistol suddenly erupted, a flash momentarily lighting up the entire trench in the increased darkness that seemed to descend immediately after.

The crash of the pistol lasted no longer than the flash, but it burrowed itself into the soul of every British soldier in the trench, and undoubtedly into the conscious minds of every German soldier within a few hundred yards of the place. Before too long, the whole bay would be infested with Germans, eager to discover who had fired a shot in the middle of the night. For, on the Western Front, it was rarely done without good reason.

Reg practically watched the bullet eject itself from the muzzle of the pistol, tearing its way along the narrow trench and whizzing past his ear. He was thankful that it passed him, but heard a thud and a clatter as it struck flesh just a short way behind him.

He turned just in time, to see Peterson spin to the floor

in agony, as the round glanced through the side of his neck, blood immediately spraying itself in every direction, as if the pressure inside had just been waiting to burst.

"I'm okay," he managed to gasp, almost as soon as he hit the ground, "it's just nicked me."

He began fumbling around inside his tunic, trying to withdraw a dressing from the inside to press tightly against his neck to stop the streaming scarlet.

As if his speech had acted as some sort of approval, every British soldier sprang into action, each one doing something to try and protect themselves as much as possible.

The Captain began stuffing papers down the front of his trousers indiscriminately, picking up anything and everything that would mean he had something to show for his latest excursion. Hughes began to ready himself at the end of the bay, bringing his revolver up to his eye line, ready to pop anything that moved in front of him. Reg did the same, standing just in front of the grimacing Peterson as he sorted himself out.

McKay had clearly needed the shot of adrenaline, as he immediately brought his bayonet up and sank it straight into the German's chest, just glancing off the breastbone as he drove it home. The German groaned and gasped, before letting out a low howl, more like a desperate plea to anyone that could hear him to help get him out.

McKay reacted instantly, cupping his hand to the German's mouth to subdue anymore noise, but it was already too late for that, the party had already begun.

Streaks of light suddenly puffed their way into the night sky, like some sort of firework display, as three flares began to sizzle away above the German frontline, blinding everyone in its vicinity for half a second.

Reg presumed it was to alert everyone to the raid, and to watch out over No Man's Land as they retreated, which was going to make their chances of survival even slimmer than they already were.

Reg realised that Peterson had fallen silent. There was no point in being quiet now, everyone knew they were there.

"Sir, Peterson, he's passed out."

The Captain barely looked up as he spoke, his strong, aristocratic tones carrying his authority even amongst disaster.

"Leave him. He's already lost a lot of blood. He'll have more of a chance if he stays here…Right everyone, we've outstayed our welcome here. Grab what you can. Let's go."

It was a testament to these young men that they didn't immediately start fighting each other for the privilege of being the first one out of the trench. Instead, they slowly made their way to the trench ladder that adorned the parapet, each one of them weapons raised and walking methodically backwards.

Earnshaw was the first up, whispering urgently to the next man to get up. Within seconds, all of them, except Peterson, had vacated the trench. Now, it was just No Man's Land that stood between them, and safety.

2

CAPTAIN ARNOLD WAS IMMEASURABLY INFURIATED. He hadn't got half of what he had gone for. Now, he was lying face down in the dirt, drinking in large amounts of muddy water, trying his absolute utmost not to get his head ripped from his shoulders by a German machinegun.

The rest of his raiding party were lying about nearby, similarly keeping their skulls as far away from the sporadic gunfire that was hindering their withdrawal. Each one of them dragged their chins through the mud, trying to find a depression in the ground or maybe even the luxury of a waterlogged shell hole that they might be able to scurry to.

Arnold began to feel the dampness of the ground slowly seep through the layers of his trousers, beginning to just kiss his skin.

That's not good. He was desperately hoping that he somehow might avoid the sodden trousers routine that he knew was inevitable. Especially as he had more pieces of paper stuffed down the front of his trousers than The Times had in Fleet Street.

He tried his hardest to shuffle the papers around as best as he could, but he could already feel them sticking to his skin and tearing as he pulled them, knowing full well that within seconds, the ink would seep into his skin too.

Captain Arnold had no idea what it was exactly that he had picked up, as he had found nothing of any real significance in the few short, uninterrupted minutes that they had had in the enemy's trench. For all he knew, Peterson had died to recover a bunch of poems and sonnets, written for a loved one back in Cologne.

It wasn't a particularly pleasant thought.

The Captain looked so uncomfortable as he shuffled around in the mud, that Reg's first thought was that he had been hit.

"You okay, Sir?" he gasped into the darkness, immediately forcing the others into a premature halt at the sound.

"All okay, Dornan. Keep moving," he growled, through gritted teeth.

Arnold came over as far more aggressive than he intended, and he thought for a moment that he caught the beginnings of a shocked tear forming up in Dornan's eye. As he went to apologise, he noticed something within himself.

He was angry.

He was angry that he had risked his life to collect up a bundle of papers that was now doing its utmost to form a pseudo-skin around his upper leg. He was angry that Peterson had stood in the way of the stray bullet that had resulted in his abandonment. But, most of all, he was completely incensed with Lance Corporal McKay.

Arnold couldn't for the life of him understand why he hadn't killed the German when he had the chance. In fact, he was an experienced enough soldier to have never let the German make it that close to them in the first place.

What had happened to him?

In the last few days, McKay had gone completely into himself, taking every opportunity that he could to be away from everybody else. It was a far cry to how he had been just a week before.

McKay was a well-liked member of the team, in fact he was probably the most popular. It wasn't because he was friendly or kind to everyone that he met, but more because of his straight-talking, to the point nature.

You always knew where you stood with McKay. For Captain Arnold, that was lower down the pecking order than the Kaiser, but for the Captain, that was just fine. He wasn't there to be liked, he was there to get a job done, to see the war through, before moving on to the next part of the world in need of the British Expeditionary Force. He had been in the Army before the war started and, he hoped, he would still be in the Army after the war had ended.

McKay took a dislike to the Captain for a number of reasons, the first being the fact that he was from a privileged background. McKay automatically assumed that made the Captain pompous and only interested in his own career progression, the latter having an element of truth within it.

But the remorse and sadness that Arnold was feeling over the death of Private Peterson, was something that was surprising even the Captain.

In the first thirty seconds since leaving the German trench, the Captain swayed from mourning for Peterson, to a downright anger towards McKay no less than four times, as his confused mind tried to process everything that had happened.

McKay was a fantastic soldier and, until tonight, a ruthless killer, so he couldn't quite understand what had caused his stage fright.

Captain Arnold didn't quite get to the end of his thought process, as his meandering mind was cut short but the solid thumps of trench mortars as they opened up, presumably a prelude to the artillery, that would take a little longer to communicate with.

The new-found urgency with which the raiding party was now required to move with, made them all begin to pull themselves up, so they could crouch and run rather than drag themselves back to the frontline.

Within seconds, another volley of flares lit the darkness of No Man's Land, so brightly that Captain Arnold's eyes ached as he tried to look away from them. They were forced back into action quite quickly as the accompanying rattle of machine guns became the only sound any of the raiders could focus on.

Each one of them flattened themselves on the ground once again, becoming an integral part of the earth as they tried to burrow themselves into the safety of the ground.

Suddenly, there was a splash, followed by an intense burst of machine gun fire, that zipped just inches over the Captain's head.

What on earth was that? Had someone taken a hit and fallen into a shell hole?

"Cap! Over here!" he recognised the voice of McKay instantly, his curt Scottish accent quite surprising to Arnold's ears after the eerie silence of the past few days.

Arnold scurried his way towards the shell hole, like a rat, whereupon he was dragged into the apparent safety of the body of water that housed all manner of creatures and diseases.

He was pleased to see that all of the remaining members of his raiding party were crouched in the hole together, each one of them still clutching on tightly to their now-defunct weapons, the range of both a bayonet and a revolver completely inadequate in the fight against a well-fended machinegun.

The flares continued to sizzle high above their heads, each one seeming to diminish with a fleeting sigh, as the remnants joined the descending arc of the trench mortar.

Captain Arnold took a brief moment to compose himself, before trying to think what his next orders might be, his loyal subjects all staring at him in the darkness awaiting his next command.

We need to move. But where to? Nowhere has better cover than here, for now. If we move then we're more likely to take hits.

His thoughts were once again interrupted by dull thuds, but not the high pitched popping of a trench mortar, but the altogether far more sobering thuds of far-away artillery. Instinctively, he lifted his head over the edge of the shell hole, just in time to see the horizon flashing away as if it was blinking at him.

About three seconds to impact.

Sliding back into the shell hole, Arnold was completely snapped from his encompassing thoughts of everything but survival.

Arnold's mind moved like lightning. He knew that they could hunker down in the shell hole and wait for the barrage to end. From experience it was a terrifying ordeal that would last about two, consistent, ground-shuddering minutes. After which they would have to deal with the inevitable German patrol that was sent out to fix the gap in their barbed wire, before trying to creep back to the British frontline as quietly as possible.

If they did that, then there was a high chance that a shell could land slap bang in the middle of the crater that they occupied, obliterating each one of them to such a degree that their body parts would be intertwined forever.

Not the nicest thought.

His mind was made up. But he wasn't certain it was the right decision.

"Move! Everyone! Up and out! Get to our lines, now!"

Sergeant Hughes leapt into action, the man being far more nimble on his toes than the aged lines that were stationed on his face would suggest.

"Out! Out! Out! Go!"

As one, they splashed around in the shell hole, expertly attracting the attention of the German machine guns, as the rattles began to resound in perfect harmony with the first impacts of artillery shells.

Mud and earth were sprayed in every direction, with such an aggression that for a moment the Captain was truly terrified about being cut down by an expeditious piece of dirt.

McKay was leading the pack, Dornan just behind him, with the Captain and Sergeant Hughes level with one another at the rear. Instinctively, they separated, keeping close to one another but not so close that they could both be cut down with a single shriek of gunfire.

Suddenly, Dornan stopped dead in his tracks, as if he

had thumped straight into a brick wall. He staggered for a moment, before crumpling in a heap on the deck, his body lifeless.

By the time Captain Arnold had reached him, Hughes was already dragging him through the dirt, and down the side of another bowl of dirty water.

Blood gushed forth from the top of his leg, just as they were coated with a fine layer of muck as they perched at the bottom of the crater.

"Where's he hit?" queried the Captain, immediately feeling the fool as he stared at his blood-stained trousers.

The Sergeant ignored the stupidity of the question and answered regardless.

"Top of his thigh, just below the hip, I think."

"I…I, I think it was a piece of shrapnel, Sergeant. I can feel something on the other side though."

Instantly, Hughes was fumbling around vigorously, ignoring the quite obvious pain searing through Dornan's body.

"It's alright, Reg," the Captain muttered pathetically, "you're going to be alright."

Hughes looked up at the Captain after rummaging around, shaking his head despondently, in full view of Dornan.

The Captain sucked his lips in for a second before defiantly ordering to patch the Private up. They both knew that it was a pointless enterprise, but one that would make Dornan's final few minutes ones of care and compassion.

McKay suddenly slid down the bowl in a storm of dirt and perspiration, just as yet another artillery salvo landed all around the hole. It was almost as if the Germans were beginning to get their eye in.

"Oh no…" he whispered as he came to a stop, whipping his woollen hat off in the process. McKay knew that the death of Peterson had been his fault, and now Dornan, the new boy, was about to bleed out, the amount of blood already seeping through the dressing on his leg was enough to tell him that.

"Are we…Do we…" his voice faded into a pathetic grumble, nothing more than saliva-engulfed crackles and croaks.

"McKay," the Captain bellowed, with little sympathy or mercy in his voice, "Get out of this hole, now. Get back to our lines and make sure they know that we're going to be coming in, hard and fast!"

It wasn't out of necessity that the Captain dismissed McKay, but more out of a selfish desire to conserve his own energy. He really couldn't be dealing with a cowering soldier right now, especially one that he blamed for the death of two of his men.

"Sir," came the grovelling reply, as he pulled his hat back on and tumbled from the hole.

"You should go too, Nicholas."

"No, thank you, Sir. As I've said before, these boys are mine as much as they are yours."

"How very chivalrous, Sergeant."

They smirked at each other in the dark, their white eyes burning ferociously against their darkened skin.

Reg Dornan began to sway in and out of consciousness, at which point, in a rare moment of coherence, Sergeant Hughes offered him a tiny bottle of brandy, one that he had had stitched into the lining of his tunic, for just such an occasion.

Dornan took it, and sipping it, fell into a deep sleep, one that he would never awake from.

The two, seasoned soldiers took a quick, knowing glance at one another, before rolling away to the far side of the shell hole and pulling themselves up and over.

It had not been a night to remember, for any of them.

3

"Stand to! Stand to!"

Groggily, I repeated the call up and down the bay, until every man that occupied the trench was perched up on the firestep, rifle ready, but heads down.

It was a call that had, at first, intimidated me, but now, as a seasoned and knowledgeable soldier, I knew full well that this was just a matter of routine, just another tick on the list of the frontline soldier.

Standing to always seemed rather a curious phenomenon to me, millions of men all waking up from their terrible sleep, waiting for the enemy to come peering out of the mist, their spectral shapes slowly taking form until they were snarling, murderous soldiers. But they never seemed to come, at least not when I was there anyway. For the first few months, I always asked myself the same question.

Why? Why did they never seem to come, when our generals were so convinced that they were?

But, after twenty, or maybe thirty more stand tos, I

slowly began to understand why. The Germans were doing exactly the same thing.

It felt strange to me that two powers, crouching in holes across Europe, would all mobilise at exactly the same time every day, mirroring one another's movements, only to shadow each other's actions as soon as the watch was stood down. It was a never-ending cycle, of standing to, weapons cleaning, then breakfast, followed by the strengthening and repairing of trenches. Day after day. Week after week.

It was why I was so ecstatic to finally get off the frontline after we had finished the morning's duties. It was our final stand to until we were slowly rotated backwards, gradually adjusting ourselves back into a short normality that would hopefully allow us a great deal of rest.

I perched myself on the firestep, next to Bob Sargent, who had been scanning the horizon with a periscope for the last ten minutes, searching for the elusive enemy.

"I can't wait to get out of here," I croaked to him, desperately pining to be able to take my hands off my weapon for twenty seconds, just long enough for a sip of water, or something a little stronger.

"Really? I'm beginning to like it here," he said, not lifting his eyes from the periscope for a moment, but his grin, which stretched from one ear to the other was blindingly obvious.

"You are so predictable, you know that?" I said, reflecting his grin as if he was staring into a glassy lake. His humour was bad, but it was what had kept me going for these last few weeks. He was the one that had taught me that you just had to keep on going, to keep plodding on. It was odd, especially as he was hardly experienced in the matter himself.

The last week had been a dreadful one, to the point where our time on the frontline had been extended far longer than any other company, on account of the fact that replacement companies could not be made up fast enough to dispatch to the frontline. So, instead, we were simply taking on replacement after replacement, to plug the gaps that were opening up with every gunshot that cracked out over No Man's Land.

As a consequence, Bob and I had spent the last two weeks consistently in the frontline trenches, only moving backwards for a few hours at a time, which were gratefully taken as an opportunity to get some sleep. Bob had worked out that meant we would have increased our chances of dying by over fifty percent, and yet, here we were, still on the stand to, grinning at one another.

"The only way of increasing our chances of copping it," he had croaked in his genteel tones, that were slowly becoming more rustic on account of his constant smoking, "would be if the brass hats decided to send us over the top. I don't think even we could survive another one of them."

He had been right, but fortunately, we hadn't been over the top since the fateful event that our whole platoon had been wiped out, bar two fools who were expected to carry on as normal. Since that afternoon, when the fresh-faced, young Captain had approached us, the wheels of change had been set in motion, and had raced along the track faster than the Scotch Express train.

We were no longer in the fifth platoon, 2 Company, 2nd Battalion of The Rifle Brigade. Five platoon no longer existed. I wasn't even sure if the second company was still in existence, for we were now the third platoon in 1 Company.

Bob and I were happy to be in a new platoon, looking forward to getting to know our men and the camaraderie that we had experienced in five platoon a couple of weeks before. But what we were met with instead, made us rethink what being brothers in arms actually meant.

The open arms with which we had hoped to have been welcomed by were well and truly shut. That was in spite of the fact that we had seen what it was like to go over the bags, and watch as an entire section, platoon and company had been decimated by artillery and machineguns. No one had made any attempt to get to know us, which in turn hampered our efforts in finding out more about them. There was something being harboured in that platoon that made it almost impossible to maintain a conversation, past the parameters of trench life.

Maybe it was because we were seen as the replacements in their section that they took offence to; these boys didn't care for experiences or achievements, they wanted their old boys back, the ones that they had most likely trained with and grown with. What made matters even more testing for both Bob and me, was the fact that we hadn't just replaced two inexperienced privates. We had replaced two of their section NCOs, popular ones at that. Our time there was doomed to fail, right from the off.

Our section hadn't seen war in the way that we had. They were still yet to go over the top in a full-scale advance and so, Bob and I had been like-for-like replacements. Bob Sargent was now a Lance Corporal, although in my mind, he deserved the second stripe on his arm as well, as they were a little too heavy for me. Until I had been awarded my stripes, I had never realised there was such a gulf between the other ranks and a junior NCO, but maybe it was just my nervous and unconfident demeanour that had seen to that.

No matter what it was that had caused the gulf, the idea that we were both 'Jonahs' of the platoon hadn't helped us settle in, in the slightest. It was something that had been harshly whispered around blacked-out trenches in the middle of the night, as if it was some ghostly tale about how the frontline was being haunted by the Devil himself. The story, although never told in the presence of either their Lance Corporal or Corporal, was nonetheless heard by them and at first, we tried to not let it get to us, but the evidence for the curse was astounding.

Men had been dropping like flies ever since we had taken over in third platoon, in all manner of ways that were imaginable, and some that weren't. Two men, I couldn't even remember their names by the end of the next day, had been killed while out repairing a section of our barbed wire, that had been torn apart by enemy artillery. Another, Private Saunders, had been taken ill with a suspected case of Typhoid, which had placed everyone else on high alert for days afterwards, convinced that we would all be in the next hospital bed that became available. Saunders died four days after he left the frontline.

Privates Hillier and Mace had been killed while returning from Company HQ with a case of supplies that had been earmarked for the exhausted platoon. What made the whole sorry affair far more harrowing was the fact that they had, in fact, been killed by one of our own shells. A round had fallen short of its intended target on the German frontline. It was just one of those things, we all had to get on with our day and breathe a sigh of relief that it wasn't us, this time.

Chalmers had been the one that had troubled me the most. In fact, since his death, his was the face that had loomed over me in every single one of the nightmares that I had begun to experience.

"Sniper!" had been the panicked calls that had been screeched all around, less than a second after the gunshot. I had awoken about a second before the shot had rung out, a weird coincidence that always occurred to me just moments before disaster.

As I sprinted towards the latrines, the enemy's favourite hunting ground for a target, all that met my gaze was an incredible amount of blood and gore, that had sprayed itself in large chunks on anything that it could stick to. Chalmers, who had been practically the only man to accept both Bob and me, was lying prone in the latrines, his body now a mess of faeces, mud and gore.

The blood had trickled into the awaiting muck below him and had produced an odd burning brown colour, as if a submerged fire had been lit beneath it and what we were seeing was the effects of the licking flames.

Private Chalmers had taken a bullet just below his eye, the force of the round ripping away at most of the right hand side of his face, which now dangled down as a piece of flimsy cloth, like that which hung to dry from a laundry line.

His eyes rolled wildly around in their sockets, as if they were controlled by a series of magnets being pulled around by some invisible puppeteer. He grunted and gasped as he tried his hardest to fight the instinct to die and I found myself simply staring at him, praying that the pain hadn't yet set in, and that he would pass away before it could take a hold of him.

More men arrived on the scene. The disgusted faces at the curse of Sargent and Ellis now complete, they carted his jerking body away from the latrines, so that he could at least die in the more pleasant surroundings of his frontline trench. He was dead before they could set him down on the ground.

I, nor Bob for that matter, believed in curses or superstition, but the overwhelming evidence that we seemed to be getting these boys killed appeared convincing. If not to us, then to the rest of the boys in the platoon, who were becoming more and more despondent as the days wore on.

We had both conferred about the possibility of being transferred, or at the very least splitting up, not for our own good but at least for the surviving members of the platoon. They thought it was us, they might stay alive if we went.

Our discussion was inconclusive however. The men couldn't stand us and we hadn't been particularly impressed with the way that we had been treated. But still, we were their NCOs, they still needed nurturing and, before too long, we were convinced that they would be sent over the top. At which point we were almost certain they would want to fall back on our experiences. We still had a duty of care to these men and even if we did put in for a transfer, there was no way of knowing whether the CO would see it as an act of treachery or desertion, which could well end up with us in front of a black cap-wearing General in the courtroom.

We knew we would die, but we were determined it wouldn't be at the mercy of a firing squad.

"So, that's that then?" asked Bob, in the final round of our negotiations between us.

"Yep," I announced, somewhat smugly that we deemed ourselves important enough to teach these young kids a lesson. "We stay here. At the end of the day Bob, as long as I'm fighting with you, I don't really care who the other men are."

"That's good," he replied, as I expected a similar sentiment to be returned, "because the way we're going, the rest of these boys will be dead before month's end."

4

"WHAT ARE you planning on doing first?" Bob asked me in between his seventh and eighth cigarettes of the day. He had got me into the habit of smoking some weeks before, but I was still not up to his standard of as many as possible before he ran out for the day.

"Might as well smoke them all as soon as possible, might be dead before I get to the end of the packet," had always been his reply when anyone had ever challenged him on his consumption.

"Huh?" I said as I began to clean the bolt of my rifle with the cleanest part of the cloth that I could find. It had become an almost hourly ritual of mine, to clean my rifle at every opportunity, so that I knew that I could depend upon it with my life, as I had so often already.

"When we move back to Le Plantin. What will you do first?"

"Sleep, most probably," I said with a snort, as I finished cleaning the Lee-Enfield by slotting the bolt back into place. "What about you?"

"Dunno really. I'd like to sleep, but I think I'll try and get a wash first. Plus, I think I have lice again, you know."

At the thought, I found myself itching away at my skin, as I so often did because of the damp fabric that had apparently tried to become a part of my skin in recent days.

"Probably for the best. I haven't been able to see your face for days now. I only recognise you by your smell."

His chortling and reply was cut short by the sound of squelching footsteps, followed by the slightly less sucking noises of feet on wooden boards as they thumped their way into the bay. The trenches had dried out considerably over the last few days, but it still lacked that final bit of sunshine to be able to get to the very pits of the holes, so much so that there was still a generous helping of glooping mud, just waiting to cake itself all over your lower leg.

The boots that arrived around the corner were filthy, but markedly cleaner than ours, which had become stained a light brown colour owing to the amount of dirt that had stuck, then dried to us, since we had been at the front. It would probably only take a matter of hours for the replacement's kit to emulate our own.

"Your replacements, boys," announced Lieutenant Harding, our CO, himself a recent replacement to the platoon. "This is, second platoon. Two Company. You lot, gather your belongings. We'll form up in Coventry Street."

"Belongings?" muttered Bob as we began to shoulder weapons and stuffing pockets with notebooks, "Nothing we have is ours!"

Fortunately the Lieutenant didn't hear him, which was just as well as he had seemed like he had wanted to make an impression since being on the frontline, trying to assert his authority in any way possible, something which annoyed the company commander very much.

"Any of you got local girlfriends?" chirped Bob, as we began to make our way to the communication trench, eliciting a few nods of heads and murmurs.

"I hope you can trust them with him around!" I suggested as we finally began to make moves away from the killing zone.

"And if one of you soppy lot cops it, do let me know. They might need a shoulder. Know what I mean?" Bob chuckled all the way back to the reserve lines, and I could imagine his hands rubbing together as he plotted his every single, lust-filled move as we made it back to Le Plantin.

We spent the next few days perched in the reserve trenches, waiting for something to happen which more often than not resulted in being another weapons inspection from the Lieutenant, which he himself admitted was done just for something to do.

The monotony in the reserve lines was awful. At least on the frontline, with all the snipers and artillery bombardments, there was something to do. Admittedly, that something quite often meant dying, but even that seemed far more fun than being in the reserve. At least there was an element of danger, excitement that kept us going.

In reserve, all we did was play cards and write letters. But, even in the monotony, the rest of the section seemed adamant not to want to talk to us past two or three sentences, no matter how hard the Sergeant tried.

"Get to know one another. Find out where they're from, what they did in the past. The better you know each other, the better you'll be able to fight. And the better you fight, the more chance we all have of staying alive. Got it?"

I knew his intentions were good, but knowing each other well, playing off each other's strengths and weaknesses, was hardly going to keep someone alive when a shell indiscriminately severed limbs from bodies, or vaporised someone into nothingness. It was futile, but I appreciated the sentiment all the same. I just stuck with Bob.

Bob slowly got into an irritating habit of trying to count the number of flares that were sent up on a nightly basis, to the point where for the first time since I had met him, I just wanted to be on my own, or at the very least, without him.

The flares would be sent up frequently throughout the night and, owing to the fact that it was far more difficult for the sharpshooters to take a shot at the reserve line, especially in the middle of the night, Bob would often have his head above the parapet. Periscope to his eyes, he would commentate on what was going on in No Man's Land, more with a childlike speculation than from anything he could actually see.

"Another patrol out tonight," he would say, his assumption often challenged. "Why else would flares be up?" would be his angry reply. It was something that I had noticed in him in recent weeks, that his tolerance of others was wearing incredibly thin. We all needed a break, but Bob needed it more than any of us.

Whenever he got into one of his foul moods, I knew that it was best to stay with him, but keep my mouth shut. So, I often took to pulling out the small, palm-sized hip flask from my top pocket, the one that had belonged to my previous Sergeant, George Needs.

Needs had been a good man, one who had taught me a lot in the relatively short time that I had known him. It was he who had been the man responsible for telling me to let go of all manner of hope and belief that I would make it home alive. It wasn't something that I had disliked him for, but something that I praised him for. If I had sat on the frontline expecting to make it home, I would have been a distracted soldier, a bad one.

I would toss the hip flask in my hand, over and over, especially when Bob set me on edge with his latest outburst. I rarely got nervous anymore, but it would always come out at the slightest hint of discomfort in my stomach.

GRHMN

George Robert and Helen Margaret Needs.

I tried my hardest to try and recall the conversation that I had with Needs some weeks ago, but for the life of me I couldn't. It had seemed so long ago now that he was slowly fading from my memory, the only things that I could recall were the words that had a direct impact on me and the way that his body was slumped over a pile of rubble in the schoolhouse, scarlet dot at the side of his head.

Bob, as he so often did, interrupted my thoughts, as he passed me a cigarette, the silent sign between us that it was our turn to man the Vickers.

Bob always liked to be the one to feed the ammunition and spot the next target area for me, which meant he always sat to my right, feeding the ammunition belt that held two hundred and fifty rounds exactly.

There was never any real prospect of being able to fire the Vickers during our four hour watch, but being up close to it, hiding behind the camouflaged sandbags that appeared to be impenetrable, gave me such an immense feeling of divine power, the ability to take life, or let a man live. I desperately wanted the chance to fire it in combat, but at the same time I feared it more than anything else in my life before. It was a weapon that had revolutionised war, it was a weapon that had industrialised it. I supposed that was why Bob never wanted to get too up close and personal with it, especially as some others, had proudly declared that they loved using it, even when it came to the point of cutting down hordes of men as they advanced upon the gun.

Before I let my mind begin to dissuade me from wanting to ever use the Vickers, Private Bushell, a red-faced dogged man who acted as the CO's unofficial messenger, came haring around the corner. His face was even redder than I had ever seen it before. He was sucking air in drastically, through his yellowing teeth.

"Corporal Ellis. Lance Corporal Sargent. The lieutenant would like to see you in his dugout, as soon as possible, please."

Although the order had come from a superior officer, Bushell had a knack of making every command come across as a request to afternoon tea, which had been taken advantage of on more than one occasion.

"As soon as possible," he repeated, before spinning round on his heel and charging from the rest of the section. Bushell was out of sight within moments, his total time in the trench with us no more than ten or eleven seconds.

Bob and I looked at each other, confused for a moment.

"He was in a hurry."

"Probably didn't want to risk being out in the open for too long. He's always been like that," Bob politely sniggered at my attempt of a joke.

"What do you reckon then? Why the dugout?"

Since we had moved to the reserve, we had all been granted with slightly more luxuries than we could afford on the firing line and, for the lieutenant, that meant he got to share a dugout with a few of the other platoon commanders, which he treated as his own.

"Don't know," I replied, honestly.

"Court Martial?" Bob asked with a wink.

"Can't for the life of me think what we might have done to warrant that, though."

"Maybe you hadn't cleaned that rifle enough," Bob suggested with a hearty chuckle.

"I reckon we're being sent back to the frontline. Maybe an advance?"

Bob shrugged.

"Either way, I reckon we won't be getting our free time in Le Plantin. Your exploits will have to wait."

Bob's face suddenly dropped, as we picked up our rifles and negotiated our way to the lieutenant's dugout. But first, we stopped to light our cigarettes.

5

"Promotion?"

It was yet another wild, unfounded guess as to the reason behind our summoning to the lieutenant's dugout, each one becoming more and more fanciful than the last.

"Bob, we were promoted only two weeks ago, they're hardly going to be stitching another stripe on our arms just yet. If they keep promoting us at that rate then we'd be generals by Christmas."

He liked that one, "Sounds good to me," he retorted in between his lacklustre chuckles.

"Medals," he announced suddenly when we were just feet from our destination. I looked up at him smirking, observing the unquenchable grin that was stained onto his face by now.

He rubbed away at his upper arm, itching at the wound that had caught him in the last advance. I knew that it was giving him all kinds of grief, along with the gushing head wound that he had sustained, but he refused to talk about it. There wasn't a single complaint uttered from his lips about the pain that I imagined to be unbearable.

"You really should go and see the Doc about that, you know."

"I reckon a couple of Distinguished Conduct Medals are heading our way, what do you think?"

"You *really* should go and see the Doc, soon. Anyway, what did you actually do to deserve the DCM?"

"Not much really. Survived, I guess."

"I don't think that really counts, mate."

We ducked our way into the dugout, a shabby little hole in the side of the trench that was partly submerged under the ground. I took two small steps downwards, before I clonked my head on the first wooden beam that had been used to shore up the ceiling of the dugout. The rest of the walls were a mixture of wooden boards and sheets of corrugated iron, rusting on account of the cold, damp walls it was holding up.

Nevertheless, the dugout was comparably luxurious, with a table and a couple of chairs, that were situated around a series of maps that littered the entire room. On the far side was a workbench-type piece of furniture, which housed a small bowl of scummy water, razor, toothbrush and other utensils that the officers used to maintain their aristocratic appearance.

"Well, I was actually a King's Scholar so—"

"Oh, you were at Eton? As was I, Lieutenant, as was I."

"Oh really? Now that is interesting. So, what do you reckon—"

"Were you in the officer training corps?"

"Why, yes I was, Sir. I was pretty good at it too, hopefully it'll stand me in jolly good st—"

"What were the two fellows name's again, Lieutenant?"

The lieutenant squirmed as he was unsure whether the figure before him was going to interrupt him once again before he had a chance to finish. The visitor to the dugout was a tall man, so much so that his head was bent at a most unnatural angle so that he could fit into the dugout at all. He was slim, but clearly had meat on his bones, more than I had ever been able to build up in my eighteen years on civvy street.

I got a flash of his sleeve as he momentarily swayed his body round, he was a Captain. Still, the conversation between the two men continued, the Captain doing a marvellous job of preventing the lieutenant from sucking up to him too much, as he never allowed him to fully finish a sentence.

It wasn't out of a discourtesy that the man appeared to do it, but more out of an apprehension, a terrifying fear almost of an awkward silence. So much so that there never was one, just an interruption after interruption.

Bob took it upon himself to make the two old Etonians aware that we were in fact here, by clearing his throat unnecessarily loudly, which seemed amplified ten-fold due to the confined nature of the room.

"Ah…gentlemen. Erm, please do take a seat." The Captain waved away our salutes, as Lieutenant Harding extended his arm out to us, offering the only two chairs in the dugout. Both the officers quite clearly comfortable staying stood up. That way, whatever they were about to tell us, would seem far more imposing than if we were eye-level. Already, they were winning.

"As you both well know, you are two of our most experienced men in the platoon and quite possibly the whole company."

"We're the only two that survived, Sir," interjected Bob quite boldly.

"Yes…well, regardless, you are two of only a handful of men in the company who have actually experienced what it is like to go over the top. I myself am still yet to find out what it is like, so I cannot imagine what you have been through, but the higher ups are greatly appreciative of what you have done."

I didn't like where any of this was headed. The fact that we had apparently been brought to the attention of the 'higher ups' was more than a little unusual, which meant that we were being picked out for something we'd done, or something they wanted us to do.

I sensed Bob glancing across at me from the corner of my eye, but I didn't return his stare. I knew we were both thinking the same thing.

Definitely no court martial. Where are the military police?

That was a bonus.

"On a personal level, I have admired you and the way that you have handled your section. I have taken note of the fact that they have not exactly warmed to you, but the professionality that you have displayed in your constant education and nurturing of the men has not gone unnoticed."

Lieutenant Harding was a worthy speech-maker, a man who would one day make great speeches in parliament, I had no doubt. But, he was preparing to say goodbye, I could sense it in his tone, which filled me with even more dread than if I had been arrested. We were about to be asked to do something that would make us follow in the footsteps of Sergeant Needs and all the others.

"Your diligence has been unwavering. And you have also helped me to acclimatise to the situation since I have been here."

I felt Bob raise his eyebrows at the word 'situation'. Maybe his parliamentary speeches would have to wait for a little longer.

"Anyway, this gentleman here," he said, turning towards the silent Captain as if we were in any doubt over who he was addressing, "is Captain Arnold."

"Terence Arnold, how are you gentleman?"

"Lance Corporal Bob Sargent, Sir," he said as he shook Bob's hand. I did similarly as he gripped my own sweaty palm.

He allowed a small smile to flick upwards on one side of his mouth, as the lieutenant seemed aghast that he would step over the officer and non-commissioned divide, as he had done. He was taking mental notes, trying to work out how to get his men to like him.

Captain Arnold was a man who possessed a curious face. The kind of face that in one moment it looks charming and handsome and in the next looks so harrowing and aggressive, that it leaves you wondering if you are even looking at the same man.

He had a ferocious fire burning away behind his eyes, like he knew how to end this war single handed, but something was stopping him, which was resulting in the fearful expression that seemed etched into his pupils.

"I have been tasked with carrying out aggressive patrols out in No Man's Land in recent months. In the last few weeks we have refined our craft somewhat and now carry out regular raids on the enemy's trenches, in order to gain intelligence and to get a better feel for their frontline.

"Our method is thus; we enter the enemy trenches to carry out the raid, killing any sentries and so forth that we come across. We then gather any intelligence, before withdrawing back into No Man's Land and onwards to our frontline. Quite simple really. Recently, we've been having a bit of trouble getting across to our lines because of enemy machine guns, so from now on, we will have a couple of the machine guns set up in No Man's Land to cover our withdrawal."

His voice was almost majestic, so perfect in fact that it sounded like it had been finely adjusted with a tuning fork. As if dissatisfied with the way that he had ended his briefing, he repeated chipperly, "Quite simple really."

We sat in an awkward silence for two or three seconds, Arnold resting on the back of the dugout wall as if he had become exhausted by his little monologue. Our position was still as unclear as it had been when we had first come in.

"And what? You want our section to cover your rogues while you're out in No Man's Land?"

The Captain's face seemed to light up momentarily at the mention of his men as rogues, but it quickly fell again, in a puzzled look that threw us all off balance.

It took a second or two more for the Captain to process what Bob had said, at which point the slight smile was back, the confused look disappearing as quickly as it had arrived.

"Oh…no, Lance Corporal. I want you to come with us. I want you to *be* one of the rogues."

We sat in a stunned silence for a few moments before he spoke again.

"Erm, both of you," he announced, waggling a finger between the two of us like he was telling us off.

"But, we've never done anything like this before. Why would you come to us?"

"Oh I know that. But it's quite simple really," he paused, rubbing his chin for a second. "You were both under Sergeant Needs, were you not?" We both nodded, confirming a fact he already knew to be true.

"He was a good man, was Needs. A terrific soldier. I know exactly what he would have taught you. Both on the battlefield and up here," he tapped his head. "I know you'll fit right in."

Unconvinced by his poor attempt at flattery, the Captain continued.

"Look…I lost two of my men the other night, and now I need to replace them. I have no time for mourning, I lose men all the time. But I want the best men that I can possibly get my hands on, the ones that I know will carry out my orders to the letter, no questions asked. It's not a pretty war, but what we're doing is a genuine attempt to cut it all short, gather genuine intelligence that can really help the war effort.

"I need men with active experience, men that I have heard performed their task well, despite the losses that occurred all around them. From what I've heard, the men here haven't exactly taken to you. Look, with my men, rank doesn't matter, neither does whether you were a pre-war soldier or a recent volunteer. All that matters is experience and, trust me, you two have experienced more in those twenty-four hours than a lot of men have in ten years in the army."

He finished his speech, as Bob and I looked over at each other, trying to read each other's thoughts. It seemed like we had the same thing going through our heads.

"Sir, thank you, but we have a duty of care to our men. We are responsible for their lives. We can still teach them a lot."

I was glad that it was Bob doing the speaking, as it somehow shifted the blame from me slightly.

It seemed like Captain Arnold and Lieutenant Harding had already prearranged their performance, as the Captain immediately took a backseat as Harding picked up the reins.

"There are others that can take your place gentlemen. The men still have a good Sergeant at the helm, and you have both taught me an awful lot about what to expect. You are needed elsewhere, you can have a much larger impact than two infantry soldiers sitting on the frontline all day. Honestly, you can. You're both good soldiers. Captain Arnold needs men like you."

"But, Sir," I found myself arguing this time, "Surely there are other men that can take our place within Captain Arnold's team. It's not like we're the only men in the army who have been over the bags. There are still plenty who survived."

Arnold sat quietly leaning up against the back of the dugout, perfectly content for the lieutenant to fight this one out on his own. It was building his character up, that was for sure.

"Now look here, gentlemen," said the lieutenant,

raising his voice forcefully, "it is not a question of what is right or wrong by the men in your platoon. It is about following orders and moving you to where the army want you. The decision has already been made."

Slightly taken aback by the lieutenant's forcefulness, Bob and I both sank back in our chairs, shocked almost that the lieutenant could turn so nasty, so quickly.

"I will, of course, be sad to see you go," he conceded, almost graciously. "But, alas, the matter is completely out of my hands. You are to leave immediately."

"Out of his hands?" muttered Bob as we were dismissed from the dugout. "How jolly convenient for him."

6

I felt guiltier than if I had seen a child leper begging on the streets of London. We were to leave immediately, which was probably for the best, judging by the pure hatred that we were subjected to at the news of our departure.

Word had already been sent to the platoon by the time we returned to the trench, to gather up the few bits of kit that we had there.

The guilt was pressing down immensely on my chest, physically restricting my breathing, but also mentally preventing me from feeling any kind of happiness or hope. This was good for me, I had been noticed by someone higher up and now I had been chosen to help end the war quicker. Maybe with my help, it could be all over by Christmas. Maybe.

Bob puffed his chest out, as if trying to rebound the guilt that compressed his own chest, and squared his shoulders as he prepared to face the rest of the platoon, the jeers and abuse already hanging silently over the trench. They avoided looking at us to begin with, which suited me just fine, as we hastily bundled together our haversacks and final bits of equipment.

I imagined that they would be remarkably happy, at the loss of not just one Jonah, but two. But my imaginings were nothing more than that, within seconds of our re-arrival in the trench, the animosity had been ratcheted up several notches.

I slung my rifle over my shoulder, as Bob began to address the remainder of the platoon.

"Look chaps," he said, as I felt my intestines tighten at the prospect of him losing his cool with them, "I know that we never really got on, but we both hope that you make it through all this. We know that we were never the same as your other NCOs, but we care for you. We didn't get a choice in all of this whatsoever. It was all out of our hands."

"Out of your hands? That's convenient for you," piped up one of them, in a haunting replication of what Bob had muttered as we had left the lieutenant. Bob ignored him, but my insides burned, as if oil was being poured through them instead of blood.

"Where are you off to exactly?" piped up Waters, one of the younger members of the platoon, who immediately drew snarling glares from the others.

"A Captain wants us to join his team. I'm not sure we're really allowed to say what. But we don't really know too much ourselves at the minute."

"Bet it's a posting back at HQ," spat Kitson offensively. "They've both become pen pushers. Couldn't even wait till after we've had our time off to scurry back to HQ, to clean the general's teeth for him."

"No, actually—"

I gripped Bob's arm, trying to prevent the eruption of volcanic substance that I could feel brewing inside of him. I was convinced that his arm was already searingly hot. He calmed down for a moment or two as he allowed his best friend to pull him back into line. Maybe this had been why I had two stripes on my arm to his one.

"You can believe what you like, Kitson. We're not taking an easy option out. We haven't put in for this or requested it. I think that you forget that we've seen more of this war than you have so far, we've actually been over the bags, unlike you."

I was surprised at how forceful I had become towards the man, direct comparisons between my own and others' war experience not normally something I dragged into an argument such as this one. Bob straightened up again, evidently quite pleased with the way in which I had shut the man down.

For a moment, Kitson appeared defeated, as he scuffed his feet on the floor, trying to rid himself of a few more flakes of clingy mud.

"It's funny how the rest of your section bought it though, isn't it? You two came through without a scratch."

This time I failed to hold Bob back and, if I was honest with myself, I felt absolutely no motivation to do so either. Kitson deserved everything that he was about to get. He was an insolent, insubordinate little man who showed no respect for anyone at all; he had spent his early years in an orphanage, before running away to try his hand at petty crime instead. It hadn't been as prolific a career as he would have hoped, he was in prison before his eighteenth birthday, now he was in a different prison altogether.

Bob flew towards him, gliding over the boards with such speed that he barely made a sound. Kitson watched the figure approach him and stood up to confront him. Wrong move.

Bob cannoned into him, slamming Kitson up against the wall by his throat, his forearm pressing firmly into the terrified windpipe of his subject, squeezing it with every second that he held him there.

"Don't ever say anything like that again, to anyone. Do you understand me? You have no idea, *no idea,* what went on when we advanced. Nothing at all. We all got hit when we went over, some harder than others. Some so hard that faces were hanging off, some that began to cry like a little girl as they begged to see their mothers for one last time. Brave men, heroic men that were turned into nothing more than moulding pieces of meat, just over there!"

He thrust his arm towards the frontline trench, causing Kitson to wince as he expected a firm fist to be thrust upon his nose.

"It's people like you who survive. The dirt of the army, the scum, the ones who have no idea how they made it through this far. The ones who do not deserve to still be breathing. Do you get that?"

I thought that both Bob and Kitson were going to burst into tears at any moment, and embrace each other like long-lost brothers, but instead all that happened was the reddening of Kitson's face as Bob pressed his forearm home even further.

Bob was right. In our experience, it had been the men who had no idea what they were doing, the ones who were merely following on behind the others that had survived. We didn't deserve to still be alive. We hadn't earned the right to fight another day, we had just been lucky, that was all.

I wondered if Kitson was getting the message.

"And, for the record," growled Bob as his tones began to soothe somewhat. The volcano was almost done with its eruption. "We did get scratched. The Corporal over there was blown up twice within twenty-four hours. He's got the scars up the side of his arm to prove it. I was pinged in the arm and took a piece of shrapnel to the head. No one comes back completely unharmed. I've still got a headache now."

As Bob finally began to calm down, Kitson's eyes continued to bulge as he struggled for air. I felt no desire to want to help Kitson, as I still despised the little man and clearly neither had the Sergeant, who suddenly appeared from behind me to take control of the situation. The lieutenant was not far behind.

"Right then, ladies. Break it up. I think you've all got it out of your systems now, don't you?"

The great, hulking Sergeant stepped up beside Bob and slowly prised his arm away, seemingly with little effort or persuasion.

"Now, whether they wanted to go or not, Corporal Ellis and Lance Corporal Sargent are leaving us. They've been asked to do something else, for someone else. I think they have earned the right to go, with our best wishes. What do you think?"

The Sergeant was a forceful man, one that commanded respect and that otherwise took a very gutsy man to do differently. As a result, he got a few muttered responses in his favour.

"Both of these men are fine soldiers. You could have

learnt a lot from them. Now, you'll more than likely have two replacement NCOs, who are no more experienced than you are. Maybe, from now on, you'll listen to men like Ellis and Sargent, and me for that matter."

The lieutenant, who had clearly stayed back until he was confident that no more fighting was going to take place, stepped forwards.

"And the next man that tries to ask questions about where these two gentlemen are going, will forfeit the entire platoon's right to rest. They will volunteer all of us to head back to the frontline. And I will make sure that everyone knows the request came from this section. You would not be popular boys."

Even the Sergeant seemed astounded at the lieutenant's revelation, shooting him a look so fierce that I thought that Harding would immediately drop down dead of fear.

"Right then, chaps," announced the lieutenant, as he recovered from his silent dressing down from the Sergeant. "It was nice to have served with you, no matter how short a time that was. I certainly learnt a great deal. I hope we'll see each other around."

"Stay safe, Sir," I said, as Bob reached out to shake his hand.

"Yeah, keep your head down."

"You too, boys."

Bob suddenly looked up at the rest of the section, raising his head as if he was Napoleon himself addressing his troops.

"Gents, I know we haven't got on that well, but it has been an honour to serve with you thus far. We will be back, we're only going because we have to, but we will be coming back here. You mark my words."

I didn't know how he could be so confident in his latest claim, no matter how much he wanted it to be true, but he spoke with such a conviction that everyone, myself included, suddenly believed that it would be the case. As he declared the words, faces lit up, not with smiles and cheers, but deeper than that, as if they were pleased that we did actually care about them. Even Kitson.

"You sounded pretty sure about getting back just then," I said, as we left to go and meet up with Captain Arnold and his team. "From what I can make out, there's nothing waiting for us with this little assignment other than a death riddled with bullet holes. You sounded like you actually had some hope left in you."

"Nope, no hope young Andrew. I've just always been good at false promises. Anyway, don't forget, they all want to put us in the ground, right?"

He chuckled heartily, as he always did and, with a superfluous wink, pulled out a small cardboard packet and thrust the small sticks under my nose.

7

When we were told to meet someone at the *Café de fleurs,* we were quite unsure about what to expect. But when we had arrived at the small, overpopulated but welcoming café, we immediately felt relieved about what may lay ahead of us.

"Shall we go inside? Doesn't look like our man is here just yet," Bob said, hopefully.

"I suppose there's no harm in it. As long as we keep an eye on the outside I'm sure they wouldn't mind us having a quick drink."

In my heart of hearts, I knew that the kind of drink that I was going to ask for would draw some odd looks, especially at ten thirty in the morning. But the truth of the matter was I had been dying for a strong drink for some time now, one of the only things that I had been looking forward to about being moved out into a period of rest. It was the one thing that had kept me going, especially as I had recently run out of the liquid that Sergeant Needs used to have in his hip flask.

Maybe I'll even be able to stock pile a little while I'm here.

To my displeasure, we didn't get so far as to order a drink from the plump proprietor who danced between tables and hopped over outstretched legs. As soon as we had stepped through the door, a slim, fair-haired young lad, older than both Bob and me but not by much, got up from his table, necking the last of his drink.

"Ellis. Sargent. Over 'ere lads."

We turned to look at each other for a moment, out of confusion at the young boy's accent but more over how he knew who we were.

"I suppose the Captain is far more observant than he makes out," I suggested as we began to stumble between tables and legs in much the same way as the café owner.

"'Ow do you do. I'm Earnshaw, Harold Earnshaw. Everyone calls me 'arry. C'mon follow me."

"Where you from, Harry?" Bob was always the one who asked the questions, whereas I was far more comfortable with just listening to the responses and making sure I didn't slip on the bare wooden staircase that seemed steeper than a vertical ladder.

"Newcastle, mate. It's the accent, isn't it? Not many of you lot of heard it before. What about you two?"

"No, I've never heard it either. Andrew?"

"I meant where are you from you daft beggar."

"Oh right, sorry. I'm from Portsmouth. Andrew here's from just along the coast, Southampton."

"Don't he talk?"

"Only when Bob lets me."

He chuckled, as he guided us over the landing,

explaining how the first two rooms were still occupied by the owner and his family, while the rest were 'ours.'

"What's the matter, gents?" asked another unrecognisable accent, from the far side of the room. "Not used to this kind of luxury?"

"No…" Bob's voice tailed off slowly.

The room was basic, with a few bowls of water laid out nicely by the far window, most of the floor being taken up with small, army issue beds making it look a little like a hospital ward. But to us, it was heaven. We hadn't slept on anything that resembled a bed for well over a month, even longer if you exclude the ones littered with lice and the previous occupant's remnants of mud.

"Even our generals aren't heartless enough to let us live in squalor. Especially when they basically ask us to die every single night," chimed in Earnshaw, the northern lad offering a pack of cigarettes round to us. He was instantly best friends with Bob, that much was clear.

The unknown accent that had called out to us belonged to one of the bodies that was dotted around the room, far older than anyone else around there, but still young enough to be part of the team, it seemed.

He wasn't of the normal stature and build that one would have expected of a Sergeant, tall and slim normally being reserved for the officers among us. But, there he was, the man with three stripes on his arm and an impeccably clean face, his nails trimmed so clinically I wondered if they had been cut under a magnifying glass.

"This lads, is Sergeant Two Pews, he's our senior NCO."

"Two Pews?" I asked as I gripped his hand, muddying his palm in the process. He didn't look too impressed and immediately grabbed a bar of soap from one of the bowls and began scrubbing instantly. At least, I thought it was soap, it had been so long since I had seen a bar that I had almost forgotten what it had looked like.

"Nicholas Hughes. Pews because it rhymes…and I was once in training for the clergy."

"But you gave up?"

"Yeah, wasn't for me."

"They kicked him out!" guffawed Earnshaw, as if the hundredth time he had retold the story had been the funniest. "He's two pews short of a parish! Get it? Sergeant Two Pews!"

I had to admit that the joke was a good one, so did Bob, although the Sergeant himself looked none too pleased with our amusement.

"Yeah, anyway. I'm the senior NCO here, this is my band of merry men. You can chuck your kit over there, on Dornan and Peterson's bed. Then get yourself cleaned up, the Captain won't like you looking like that round here."

I was troubled by the way that he had talked about the two vacant beds in the middle of the room; Dornan's and Peterson's. I wondered if he was as flippant about all the men that he had lost during this war, or whether it was more of a requirement of these boys to simply accept it and move on due to the nature of their work. I knew from experience that every man that I had lost in my short time as Corporal, had felt like another millstone on my shoulders, but this man seemed to be completely unaffected by it at all. I doubted he had the nightmares that I had come to know in recent weeks.

I stared at his face, impossibly clean but still dirtied with great shadows that were caused by the deep razor cut valleys that stretched out all over his face. He was older than all the rest of the men here, which was normal for a Sergeant, but his face seemed to have aged far quicker than the rest of his body had done.

He was probably in his late twenties, which, this close to the frontline made you feel closer to a hundred than it did to any of the replacements who were coming through in recent weeks.

I pondered as to what this man might have seen, that had made his face apparently age in such a premature way. It was possible that he had already seen enough of this war, and that before too long, my face would be heading in exactly the same direction. I wondered if he had been one of the thousands of men who had been sent here as soon as war had been declared and had consequently been part of the bitter fighting that had ensued in the first few months of the war.

"You been out here long?"

"I was here about a fortnight before Ellis. Guess I've been here a little under three months now. You?"

"Been here from the start. I was at Mons," that explained the deep ravines on his face then. Mons had been a heavy fight, it had led to a lot of lads signing up in my home town, that was for certain.

"You've seen quite a bit then?"

"I've seen enough. Yeah."

He stopped for a moment of contemplation, rubbing at the lines across his forehead as if he was trying to stretch them out and elongate them. Maybe that's how they'd become so pronounced in the first place. It didn't take him long to perk back up though.

"Anyway…you've met the Captain then?"

"We have."

"Good, good. He's a good man, very fair. But he doesn't like it if he has half-hearted volunteers. If he gets a whiff of the fact that you've gone off the idea of what we do here, you'll be out quicker than if he found out you were a German spy. Got that?"

"We didn't volunteer anyway," scoffed Bob.

"None of us did, lad. But, after your first one, that's it. You realise you're hooked. You learn to enjoy it. This is war, but to us, it's a game. The Captain's very sure of what we're doing here, so don't disagree with him. Just go along with it, even if you're not keen on the way he does things. It'll more than likely keep you alive.

"Besides, that's what the aristocracy want from the likes of us, isn't that right Fritz?"

He looked over the final unintroduced figure in the room, giving him a jesting knock on the back of his head.

"Fritz?"

"Yeah, this is Lance Corporal Christopher McKay. But we all know you as Fritz. Don't we, Fritzy?"

The young man, probably not even out of his teenage years yet, seemed like he needed coaxing out of his introverted state, as he simply lay on his bed watching the events of the day, not wanting to disturb the dynamics too much.

There was a strange look in his eyes though, one that told me that there was something behind his quiet exterior that was troubling him, a secret or a fault maybe that he did not want to share with the rest of his section.

Even though he was lying on his bed, I could tell that he was far shorter than all of the rest of us and I guessed that he would probably come no higher up than my shoulders if we were to stand side by side.

But what he lacked in height, he more than made up for in width, his arms alone probably the size of my humble torso in comparison. He looked like a born fighter, his body sculpted to the degree where he would be able to take seven or eight punches to the gut and not feel a thing.

His knuckles were cut and badly bruised, an array of blues and purples that extended halfway down his fingers on both hands. He clearly knew how to fight his way out of a corner.

"It's because I speak good German. Better than all these dunderheads around here."

His accent was easy to pick out, straight away. He was Scottish. His curt, sharp tones unmissable and one that matched his physique perfectly.

"My Da used to be a gamekeeper for a family up in Scotland. Got a lot of wealthy Germans up there who didn't know which way round to hold a gun."

"Shame they've learnt pretty quickly from what I've seen," I remarked, drawing a painful smirk from underneath McKay's darkened character.

"Not only that," babbled Sergeant Hughes, "but he hates our officers even more than the Hun do. He's our very own Fritz."

"Does that extend to Captain Arnold?" I innocently probed.

There was a moment of silence, where I sensed that I had asked a completely inappropriate question and one that no one wanted to answer, with all eyes falling on McKay to say something.

"No…Arnold is a good man. An excellent soldier. I owe him my life actually."

"We probably all do in fairness," hinted the Sergeant, "he's a good leader…anyhow, that's Fritz, our little human artillery…small but utterly deadly," he gave McKay an encouraging slap on the shoulder and squeezed it tightly, as McKay bewilderingly began to fight back what appeared to be tears.

As if he had been waiting outside of the door, making sure we all made our introductions and sang his praises, the Captain strode into the room optimistically. In a flash, the mood in the room changed to one of buoyancy.

"Right chaps, I hope you've all got to know each other a little bit. Get some sleep for now, our services are not required tonight. Oh, and Two Pews?"

"Sir?"

"Apparently some mail came in yesterday, will you try and find out where ours got to later on?"

"Certainly Captain."

"Thanks. I'll need to write to Dornan and Peterson's folks first thing. I'll let you have it when you go."

At the second blasé mention of our predecessors' names, I felt my intestines tighten as if they were in some sort of a vice. I wasn't going to be able to sleep very well if I had them on my mind all night.

I would have to brush them aside, just like their comrades had done.

8

THE NEXT MORNING I awoke feeling fresher than I had ever felt, my first piece of proper rest since leaving the trenches a sheer delight to my battered and bruised body.

I dreamt of all the boys that had been killed in my first few months in France, not one of them tormenting me or haunting me, but simply there, before I woke up to realise that they had gone. Some of their faces were blurred slightly now, I had seen so much death that I could barely remember who had been killed and by what, never mind recall faces or even names.

I refused to open my eyes for a few minutes more, as I drank in the relative silence compared to the never ending noise that I had been forced to endure while out in the trenches. From where I lay, I could still just about make out the faint booming of the artillery pieces opening up, on both sides, but they were miles away, and trained on the frontline as opposed to the *Café de Fleurs* that had been my resting place.

I had become so accustomed to the constant noise of

shells dropping from the sky, marksman's bullets thwacking into sandbags and the unceasing bad jokes and conversation in the sopping frontline, that I almost began to miss it as I lay on my bed. So much so that I actually found myself straining to hear something, anything that might set my mind at ease, to give me the comfort that I could take from the whistling of an incoming shell.

"Come on, get up," a voice suddenly said, louder than a shell bursting had ever done, which was accompanied with a forceful thump to my ankle. Slowly, begrudgingly, I did as the voice told me, opening my eyes just a fraction to let in a stream of light that filled them up with water immediately.

As the water began to drain itself, my vision cleared and I immediately saw three members of the section standing over the end of my bed, as if I had been comatose for so long that they were holding some sort of bedside vigil.

Earnshaw and McKay both stood behind Sergeant Two Pews, as he began to roughly shake on Bob's leg to get him up too.

"C'mon you two. Anyone would have thought you'd had a rough couple of weeks or summat."

"What's happening?" I said, reaching for some water to clear my arid throat with, gulping down the lukewarm mixture while we all waited for Bob to catch up.

He grunted, as he shot up to sit upright, surprised to see all the faces grinning back at him expectantly.

"Come on sleeping beauty. We're wanted."

"Where?"

"HQ laddy. Get dressed, it's midday."

I rubbed my eyes as the Sergeant began to get itchy feet at the fact that the new boys were taking their time.

"I hope you two don't take this much time in the Boche line, otherwise we'll be for the chop."

"What do HQ want?"

"Not sure," the Sergeant replied, his drooling therapeutic tones wafting around inside my head like a lullaby. It was probably for the best that he hadn't made it into the clergy, as his congregation would undoubtedly have been asleep inside the first ten minutes. Maybe that's why he got kicked out.

"We've learnt to stop asking questions now," McKay jumped in, "but it's probably the latest idea to add to the divisional orders book they're working on."

"Yeah. It's new and improved for this year," added Hughes jovially, "what's it called again, Harry?"

"One hundred and one ways to die on the Western Front," Earnshaw said as the three of them erupted into fits of childlike giggles.

"I like it...I like it," Hughes said in between hearty laughs, eventually having to wipe the tears away from his eyes. "You got to laugh, boys. But you end up crying anyway."

They began chuckling again, this time McKay finding the joke a little less entertaining than the other two. There was something about him as he stood at the end of my bed, a matter that was hidden behind his face that was forcing him into smiles and frowns more frequently than a pantomime mask. He wasn't quite as optimistic as the other two.

"Anyway, let's get going ladies."

∾

The room that we were guided to was packed with khaki, every single uniform crystal clean and brand spanking new. I knew that it wasn't down to a lack of action that these boys had new uniforms, but because of the sheer aggravation that they put them through, night after night.

Bob and I had been given our own new uniforms and, after dirtying the soap as much as possible, we almost looked half presentable. I was surprised to see a scar on the back of Bob's neck, which had been concealed perfectly by the thick, three-week-old grime that was plastered across his body. It was twisted and jagged, winding its way across the base of his skull like a demented river. It was a fleshy scar, the kind where you knew it had, and was still, causing great discomfort to the owner. He had had a lucky escape; he had lost a lot of blood and it could have been far more serious than it had turned out. In the event, he was back from the aid station within a couple of hours; I had been totally lost in the few moments that I had spent without him.

The room was dotted with various different groups, each section clearly content with only their immediate company and not wanting to mix or antagonise with any of the other groups.

"Everyone seems to be here," grumbled Hughes, as he flashed a wave to another Sergeant on the far side of the room.

"Alright, Harry," muttered an old looking Corporal as he took a knee by Earnshaw's ear. "Got any more of that—"

"Blimey, not 'ere George. What you trying to do, get me court martialled?"

"Sorry Harry. I'll speak to you after, yeah?"

Harry nodded as he looked over at us bashfully, "Just a bit of unofficial business. Nothing to worry about."

At that moment, the entire room seemed to stand to attention, at which point Bob and I resolved that we should do likewise and shot to our feet, a great bolt of lightning zipping up the backs of my legs as I did so.

"As you were gents," bellowed a deep, throaty voice from somewhere, his face only appearing once the sea of upright soldiers began to find their chairs.

The voice belonged to a Major, an older man in his early fifties, with a greying moustache that looked like it was beginning to rot. His skin wasn't in much better condition, the dried-out leather look clearly gaining ground across the whole of his face.

Behind him, came Captain Arnold, the complete opposite of the senior officer before him; clean shaven, young, energetic. He stood tall above the handful of other Captains that were present.

"It's good to see so many of you back here again, chaps."

Shouts of "You too, Sir!" littered the room, with a general grumble of appreciation for the Major who stood before us all.

"As most of you will know by now, the little jolly out into the Hun line the other night did not go entirely to plan. I want you to know that I do not blame you for this. If things always went to plan, then we would have been home by now. But, unfortunately, the task that you were given therefore still stands. A repeat operation will take place tonight. Captain Arnold."

"Thank you, Major Stephenson. As the Major said, we failed to meet our objective the night before last. We didn't go back last night so that we could recoup and rest. The mission tonight remains largely the same, but for the benefit of those who were not with us before, and for the slow among us, like you Norton, I will go over the plan again."

Norton and his band of rogues began jostling him around in their group of five, the subject blushing a bright shade of red in the process.

"We will head back over to the German frontline tonight. Our objective is to procure at least one enemy prisoner, for means of identification."

"So the generals know what regiment we're actually fighting," rasped Earnshaw, for the benefit of us amateurs. "Apparently they haven't got a clue."

"Wire cutters will leave the frontline at twenty-three thirty, to be at the wire by zero hundred hours. Once done they will fall back to the frontline, passing the raiding parties who will leave our frontline at the same time. Raiders will go in at zero one hundred hours and will have approximately ten minutes in the frontline, before the artillery is due to come in. You chaps are to fire just beyond the German frontline and on our flanks to contain them, from zero forty-five hours, to keep the Hun's heads down, that okay with you?"

He looked over to a segment of the room, clustered around in an outwardly facing circle, each one of them nodding eagerly at his order. They must have been the gun commanders.

"Artillery will fall on the frontline at zero one twelve. Zero one twelve. Anyone left in the frontline at that time, expect to get an almighty headache.

"Parties will withdraw at zero one ten. Make it back to the machine guns by zero one fifteen, as they have been given instructions to hit anything that moves from then on. Have you lot got your positions?"

"We took a look this morning, Sir. Same positions as last time; four guns, four shell holes. You won't miss us."

"The Vickers will be firing for ten minutes, after that you lot get out of there as quickly as possible. Then it's a good night's sleep all round after that. Questions."

There were none, except I had one burning in the pit of my stomach, that I daren't ask in a room full of bloodthirsty men and cut throats.

Do I have to go?

And the one that was even more pressing on my mind.

How will I survive?

I couldn't wait to get back to the *Café de Fleurs* and, as soon as we were back, I was rummaging around in my kit trying to find some kind of solace. I needed a peace, a reassurance that I knew I was going to be okay. I had never found that comfort from anyone other than my first Sergeant, George Needs.

I whipped the hip flask from my old tunic and began tossing it and turning it over in my hands like I had done on so many other occasions, as if some of Needs' advice and experience might rub off onto me.

Before the flask, I had my dad's old coin from South Africa, now in the hands of a Frenchman somewhere who had offered to top up the flask in return. It had tasted horrible, but it had been enough to keep me going, enough to make me feel like Needs was still beside me, offering me the harsh advice that he so often doled out.

GRHMN.

I pulled it to my lips, willing the last, slow moving droplet to just settle on my tongue so that I could feel its horrific burning that had turned into my only source of solace.

Nothing came, it was bone dry. Instead, I had to settle for the warming feeling that it spread over my palms as I continued to rotate it round and round, until I became so fed up with it that I nearly launched it to the other side of the room.

"Nothing left?"

I hadn't noticed Earnshaw entering the room, as I had been staring at my hands, bewildered at the constant quivering that had seemed to have taken hold, like an earthquake that was only affecting my fingers.

"I can get you something to stick in there, if you like. And I'm not on about water."

I looked at him for a moment, perplexed.

"That bloke. The unofficial business? I know more than one person that would want to fill that up for you. I can have it done for you by tonight, if that's what you're hoping for. On the house…this time," he charmingly quipped, with a wink. "I know someone who owes me a favour."

Instinctively, I tossed the flask to him, blindly trusting the man that was clearly in with the wrong crowd.

"Tastes awful, mind. Like that old lamp oil that some people still have lying around, you know? Paraffin. The frogs seem to like it though, never too happy to give it away, but they can't resist me sometimes."

Another wink.

He rolled the flask over in his palm, in much the same manner that I tended to do, before his eyebrows furrowed slightly when he looked at the initials. It wasn't a look of curiosity as to why I was carrying a flask bearing someone else's initials, but it was one of recognition. He had seen it before.

He pulled his gaze away from the initials, "Paraffin, mate. You sure?"

If it tasted like paraffin, then it was bound to be good enough for me. I didn't exactly have a refined palette when it came to this sort of thing.

"Either of you seen McKay?" the Captain said, before he'd even finished entering the room.

"Fritz? No, I haven't seen him since we left the briefing."

"Get him to find me if you see him. I need to talk to him urgently before we head out tonight, it'll be best for all of us."

9

I FOUND it difficult to fill my face and smoke as rapidly as the other men were. There was an uncertainty in the pit of my stomach, one that was prewarning me that any liquid or solid that I shovelled down my throat would quite quickly be brought back up again in a bile that would burn my nostrils.

Even Bob was finding it easy to pile mouthful after mouthful down his throat.

"C'mon Andrew, eat up. Could be your last meal."

That was the exact reason why I was finding it so hard to eat. I knew that there was a very good chance that I wouldn't be coming back to this café again, my brightest prospects being that I ended up in a hospital bed riddled with bullet holes and shrapnel. I wasn't convinced that everything that was planned was going to be able to come together with the same certainty of the Captain.

Bob shoved another bit of bully beef into his mouth, his chewing so loud as he spoke that it was almost enough to bring up the bile without pushing any kind of food down my throat.

"Here, Harry, what's with McKay? I know I don't really know him, but he seems…off?"

"That's just the way he is, I'm afraid. Plus, he's had a few problems as of late. But we don't really talk about them."

"What problems?" I blurted, wanting to make sure I knew everyone's weaknesses before we left, on the off chance that knowing them might actually keep me alive.

"The boss doesn't want us to talk about it…but it's probably fair for you to know. He's been struggling to fight recently. He was always good, but the last two times that we've been out, he's messed up, like he's been preoccupied with something else."

"Then why doesn't Arnold just kick him out?"

"He's not like that. He's fiercely loyal to each of us. Including you. He knows that if he tries to kick McKay out of this team, he'll need a damn fine excuse to make him avoid a firing squad. He just freezes see, any other man would call it cowardice, but not the Captain, he genuinely cares for McKay. He's trying to help him."

"Isn't that just likely to get us all killed?"

"No. The boss is good. He'll make McKay alright again. Don't you worry."

I was beginning to think that the rest of this section's blind faith in the Captain was completely unfounded. If he could fix McKay, then surely he would have been able to do it without dragging the rest of us out into No Man's Land? Plus, it was a fact that was still yet to be acknowledged that two men had been killed on their last outing and

I was beginning to get the impression that it was all down to McKay.

"The two other blokes, the ones that bought it, was that because of McKay?"

"No," he said forcefully, as he slammed his cutlery on the table and stopped what he was doing. "We are not individuals out there. Dornan and Peterson died because of all of us. We look out for each other, not ourselves. You got that?"

He pointed an accusing finger at the both of us, which was hastily withdrawn as the Captain strolled into the room.

"McKay's gone walkies again it seems. Anyone seen him?"

"Last I saw of him Sir he was upstairs, writing a letter to someone," called the Sergeant, from the far side of the room.

"I didn't know he could write."

"Don't think he can, Sir. He was very guarded when I tried to peek over his shoulder," Sergeant Hughes spoke carefully, as he dragged the razor gently over his skin, keeping his smooth face as barren as possible. It was all he seemed to do when he had a spare moment.

"Are all you Yorkshiremen as nosy as you, Sergeant?"

"How do you think we learned how to make those puddings, Sir?"

His chuckling resounded all the way up the stairs, while I finally resolved that, if I was to die, it would be on a full stomach. Picking up a tin of bully beef, I began to tentatively slide some of it down my throat, making myself feel even worse as I waited for the gag reflex to kick in.

"What did you do before the army?" Bob questioned Earnshaw as we sat and ate.

"Not a lot. I'm the most boring here, you'll soon find that out." I found it odd how unwilling the boy was to speak about himself, as he was more than forthcoming on pretty much every other topic of conversation that was available. There was something behind his cocky exterior that was altogether different, mysterious almost.

"The Captain for example. Now, he is a special type of Englishman. Both his parents are nobility, and apparently his mother is related to the monarchy by some distant relation that goes back to the seventeen hundreds. Monarchs that conveniently are well past my kind of education. But the Captain's actually the earl of some place. I forget where.

"He's also very intelligent. Likes to think. One of those people, you know? I don't get the appeal myself. But I reckon he's for parliament one day. What do you think?"

"He's got the voice," I blurted, a bit of bully beef spinning from my mouth.

"Na, he hasn't got the aggression, in my opinion," Bob fumbled, doing everything he could to make sure he didn't repeat my bad manners.

"Oh, you wait. Just you wait. He's got the aggression alright."

At that moment, the Captain appeared, as if he had a sixth sense that he was being spoken about, the look on his face one to say that he didn't like it one bit. McKay tumbled down the stairs behind him.

"Come on then gents, I think it is about time that we got a move on. What do you say? A little outing to the

Boche frontline sound up your street? Finish your food and let's go and tool up."

We finished our last few mouthfuls and instinctively went for our rifles, which drew a laugh from everyone else in the room. We'd clearly been set up, they had all been waiting for it.

"Leave them here, son," Sergeant Hughes stepped forwards so that he didn't have to raise his timid little voice too much. "They are far too clunky to be taking over there with us. We've got some others for you to try out."

"Why'd you let us spend all afternoon cleaning them then? We thought we were going to need them!" Bob exploded, which only added to the other's enjoyment of the situation, the Captain especially.

"Don't know. Thought you just got some sort of a kick out of doing it."

"I'll kick you in a minute."

"Come on, soppy," roared the Sergeant, as he began to cough and retch so much from the apparent hilarity, that I thought we would see a lung at any moment.

"You see," Hughes began to explain as we all walked out into the streets, "those kind of weapons aren't good enough for what we do. We tried to take them, the first few times. But they're simply too heavy, too long and too loud for what we do. Some people still take them, to help us out if we get in trouble, but you learn that, if we do get in a sticky patch, our best weapon is to simply run as fast as possible."

We stepped out of the café and into a cobbled square, with wide sweeping roads branching off in every gap between buildings that it could find, like some sort of leaking liquid. Apart from the sea of khaki that swarmed around and the faint thud of artillery, you could hardly tell that there was a war on.

A few locals trotted by, trying their hardest to sell their wares to the soldiers that had festooned their village in recent months. I thought it was odd that there wasn't a single French soldier around, this village seemed to be entirely British for some reason.

I stared at the statue that was just off centre in a small raised plinth surrounded by benches, transfixed by the figure that stood atop the concrete pillar, his sword drawn from his sheath and raised high above his head.

"Saint Michael the Archangel," quipped Hughes as he turned and caught me staring at the figure.

"The patron saint of warriors," added Earnshaw, getting in there before Hughes could.

"I don't really go in for all that stuff," I rebuffed quickly, not wanting a sermon from the clergy-in-training. "I just like the statue."

"Neither do I," Earnshaw timidly said in his childlike tones, as he threw another wave to a soldier he presumably did business with. I wondered if he was the man that had filled my hip flask for me. "But it doesn't hurt, just in case."

"He's also a saint of the sick and wounded, you know. Apparently, he appeared in several visions to stop various epidemics many centuries ago now, hence the sword. You never know, it might come in handy, especially if tonight goes wrong."

We walked the rest of the way in silence, each one of us deep in our own thoughts and content to be so. If tonight did go wrong, and we ended up dead, it would be nice to know that we had had a few minutes to ourselves, like before the war, where we didn't have to live every minute of every day with a group of other blokes. I tried to think back to the last time that I had been on my own, and couldn't come up with anything conclusive, but supposed it must have been back in my basic infantryman training, where the latrines had been more substantial than a little trench for five men to squat over at any one time.

It took us another five or so minutes for the others to lead us to our destination and, the closer we got, the more infrequent Earnshaw's embarrassed waves and 'hellos' became. As we took a right up another side street, I realised that, for the first time in a while, we appeared to be the only ones in khaki on this street, the only other occupants were the French civilians themselves, chatting away on doorsteps to one another, which soon came to an abrupt halt as they saw us round the corner.

As we marched up the street, I noticed the giant beads of sweat that were now streaming down the back of McKay's neck, rolling their way down and onwards to the base of his spine. His right hand was drumming on the side of his leg, as if he was pace marking his own steps. His left was lifted to his mouth, presumably so he could nibble on the remnants of his nails as he mulled over the next few hours in his head.

I became increasingly concerned about his demeanour. McKay was an experienced raider and yet, here he was, the epitome of an anxious man, not able to speak or look at anyone out of fear. I only hoped that he was able to step up when the time came. The others seemed to have some confidence in his abilities, which afforded me little assurance as I looked at him.

What worried me the most was the fact that I identified

with him fully. He was a quiet, introverted individual, only speaking up if he was directly spoken to or he knew he wasn't going to be ridiculed for what he said. He got nervous often and frequently took himself away from the rest of us to be alone, so much so that the Captain always seemed to be on the lookout for him.

The thing that concerned me the most however, was that I was exactly like him. Apart from the vast geographical difference between Scotland and Southampton, we could have been brothers, twins even.

He was a good soldier, the others had assured me of that, but there was something niggling away at him. A fear? A mistake he had made? I didn't know which, but it concerned me that someone who was held in such a high regard by his companions could be so nervous, which set me on edge no end.

"Right, welcome to the raider's paradise, lads."

"Ellis, Sargent," Captain Arnold marched his way over to us as the others began to bound around like vultures descending on their prey. "We take no webbing, nothing that chinks or chimes. Nothing that might make any obvious sounds, empty everything from your pockets that can make such a noise. You can pick them up from here when we return. You can trust the QMS here."

The Quartermaster Sergeant was an ancient looking man, who quite clearly had had enough of this war before it had even begun, he had seen far too much in his quarter of a century in the army than he cared to recall. But he seemed like a decent enough bloke, enough at least for the others to empty their pockets of cigarettes, matches and even money.

I felt uneasy with dumping the contents of my pockets

with this man, not least because of the hip flask that I had just topped up. I intended to keep it on my person at all times, it was the last bit of Sergeant Needs that I had that would keep me company.

"When we're over there, we need weapons that are light, small and highly effective. Quite a lot of what you will see will mean you will need to get up in the enemy's face. It's barbaric, but such is war. It's all quite simple really."

It had been a number of hours since I had last heard his catchphrase, but the annoyance that I usually felt when he uttered the words was completely dispelled by a fear and desperation that I felt when I saw the others begin to pick up their weapons.

All of them grabbed at revolvers, clicking the barrels forward, checking everything was clear before loading them with rounds with the nimblest of fingers.

The Captain himself picked up an old and battered wooden baton and twirled it in his hands for a few moments, before looking over at our astounded faces.

"Gifted to me by a friend in the police force. Never knew it would come in so useful."

Hughes picked up what appeared to be a similar baton, but instead of the smooth, varnished surface of the Captain's, it had great nails hammered into place, with the heads sawn clean off and sharpened to the point where it looked like it could cut through concrete.

Earnshaw selected what appeared to be a standard entrenching tool, the end of which had been sharpened to a point that could do some serious damage if it was to be jabbed into someone, but equally if the wide spade-like head was simply cracked over the back of someone's skull.

It was McKay who had surprised me the most however, as he began to excitedly look upon what was quite clearly his very own weapon. He caressed the handle as if it had been his first love and gazed upon it in much the same way. As he picked it up, my suspicions were confirmed. McKay's chosen weapon was a hatchet. Nothing more than an axe used to fell woodland trees.

I looked across at Bob, whose look of utter horror matched my own. I couldn't imagine the kind of bloodshed that would ensue if just one of these awful weapons was called into service. I much preferred a rifle, at least that way you could stay more than an arm's length away from your victim.

"Come on, chaps. Pick what you want. Take a revolver too, but only for use in emergencies. If you can, secure some jam tins in your pockets. We'll need to make a bang."

I picked up a revolver, clinking the rounds into the chamber and shoved a jam tin into a satchel that I placed on my back. The last thing that I picked up was a trusty rifle bayonet. I knew how to use one, albeit when it was fixed onto a wooden extension of my own arm, but I felt more comfortable with a swift glance to the chest than a spiky cosh over the head. Bob picked the same.

"Right then, everyone. Seems like we're ready. Let's move to the frontline."

10

It hadn't taken us all that long to move back to the trenches, as they never seemed to be all that far away wherever you were in France. As we trudged through the ever-deepening trenches, slowly becoming more complex and heavily fortified the closer we got to the fire bays, I drew more than I perhaps should have done from the stainless-steel hip flask that felt like it was now part of my own skin.

"Looking forward to being back in the fray?" Earnshaw was far too happy for an occasion such as this, and I pictured how infuriating he must have been at the news of a family bereavement or some such declaration.

"I could have done with a bit more rest, to be honest. Two weeks on the frontline with only one good night's sleep, probably not going to help anyone."

"You are a cheerful bark this evening, aren't you? Come on! Get this one right and we'll be one step closer to victory!"

"Head down Berkeley Street and then onto Fife Road, Sergeant. We'll stop there for a while."

Fife road. I recognised the name.

I shot a quick look over at Bob. He had the same expression on his face, faint recognition tinged with confusion. Then, I realised why I had recognised the name.

"Oh, here they are!"

"When you said you were coming back, we didn't think it would be this soon!"

Lieutenant Harding and the rest of the platoon stood up from where they were perched and looked up from their playing cards or notebooks. For some reason, they actually looked quite pleased to see us. Maybe it was because they knew that we were probably going to get ourselves killed tonight.

"I never go back on a promise!" called Bob, which was met with a few half-hearted laughs.

"I hope it goes all okay tonight chaps," Harding said as he spoke to us in a low voice, trying to sound far more grown up than he was. "The Captain, how is he? Is he feeling confident?"

"He doesn't really feel anything if truth be told. He's a very hard book to read."

"Yes…I got that impression when I met him. An enigma of sorts…What time is kick off?"

"About two hours, Sir. We're staying here for about an hour and then I expect we'll move up again. Don't want to be on the frontline any longer than we can help."

"Yes, quite. Well, make yourselves at home," he said, raising his voice to include the rest of our new section.

We sat in a near-perfect silence for around an hour, sipping at water, smoking cigarettes and only speaking when Sergeant Hughes continually asked us if we were doing okay.

I wondered why he did it, as there would be no tangible change in my mentality between the quartermaster's stores and the frontline. I was convinced that I was going to die and that was that. I expected he did it out of a sense of duty, but maybe also out of his own fear, seeking a reassurance from his men that he could trust them enough to back him up.

A group of rowdy men dressed the same as we were; no webbing, no caps other than a large woollen sock over their heads and no conventional weapons to speak of.

"Don't die out there!" called out Earnshaw, as one of them turned and recognised his heckler.

"If I do, there's only one person I'm coming back to haunt! Watch your back Harry!"

I was inquisitive.

"Who were they?"

"They're going in to soften the Germans up a little bit. Give them a bit of a shock."

"What do you mean?"

"Well, the Germans don't have the best rations, you see. Meaning, they don't get as much meat as us. We have bully beef, don't we? And they like a bit of the old bully. So, over the last couple of weeks, those chums have been heading out to a sap that they built about a hundred yards from the German line. Then, they've been lobbing ten or fifteen cans of bully over to our German friends."

"But why?"

"Well tonight is the grand finale. Twenty cans are going over tonight. But only ten are full of beef. The rest are jam-packed with gunpowder, nails, ball-bearings, old casings, the lot. Anything really that might cut them up a bit."

"That's a bit strong isn't it?"

"It's war, matey. Want to beat the barbarians you've got to be barbaric."

McKay was staring at the ground, shuffling his feet dejectedly, as he quickly tried to bury the tears that had fallen to the ground, in amongst all the mud and dirt.

"Oh, come on, Fritz," Earnshaw said, slapping him on the back. "They'd do exactly the same to us if they had the brains."

McKay seemed frail, like he would take one step out into No Man's Land and instantly collapse as if he was a small twig.

"Lads, time to cork up."

Sergeant Hughes appeared with a tub of grease and blackened cork, which he proceeded to hand out, to rub into our pasty faces.

"I hate this bit," Earnshaw said between his fingers, smearing a nice piece of black right across his nose. "It's a good job there are no girls around here, otherwise you wouldn't see me near this stuff."

"Do shut up, Earnshaw. Focus on what we're about to do, would you?" the Captain glanced at his watch. "The wire cutters will be setting out around about now. Nearly show time, chaps."

11

THE HIP FLASK was still twiddling around in my palms, as it had been for the last hour or so. I tried my hardest to keep it hidden from Captain Arnold, as I was concerned that he might simply toss it away at the first sight of the contraband equipment. I decided that I would try to argue that it was a weapon of sorts, able to give a German a good bash over the head with it, if that's what it came to.

I tried hard to resist sipping from it. I knew that if I took too much, then by the time it came to up and over the ladders, that my world would be swaying faster than if I was in a spinning top. I realised that I had started to rub it, as if some of Needs' experience might rub off on me in some ways. I was convinced that it had given him some sort of good luck; he had it for many years and had seen plenty of action with it in his pocket, and he hadn't been killed. But when he let go of the flask, and gave it to me, he was killed, and I survived. There was something in that hip flask that told me I wasn't quite prepared to go over the top without it just yet.

"What's the time?" I edged my way closer to Lieutenant Harding, so that I could hear his response. My own watch had been handed over to the quartermaster, and Harding was the only man that I knew right now who was still wearing one, aside from the Captain who appeared far too locked in his own thoughts to have even heard what I had to say.

"It's eleven fifteen, old boy. Getting a little bit excited now, are we? All raring to go?"

He had absolutely no idea what it was like to head into No Man's Land, to know the feeling of imminent death, only for a sudden reprieve at the last moment. His experiences of this war had been in the comparative safety of a trench, where the only thing he had to dodge was the occasional artillery shell, where rats and lice were all you saw of the enemy.

I tried not to feel any malice towards the man, as his own ignorance of the situation was through no fault of his own. He seemed like a decent enough fellow, full of the kind of youthful optimism that would see him volunteer for anything and everything, without even giving a second thought to what life outside of the sandbags might be like.

I couldn't help but lie through my teeth, I didn't want to dampen his enthusiasm.

"Yes, Sir. I can't wait to get back at them for what they did to my other platoon."

"Brilliant. What an excellent mindset to have. I'm sure you'll be terrific."

"Thank you, Sir."

We fell into a silence once again. I was beginning to enjoy them, the brief moments of utter calm that preceded the impending storm. For a moment or two, I was even able to block out the faint rumbling of artillery some miles away to the south.

I hoped that the guns that were being called into service tonight would be reliable, as I started to think about what the boys in the field artillery would be doing right now. I supposed that they were doing much the same as me, just waiting, probably in silence, as they thought through their duties in minute detail.

"Come on then, chaps," crackled the Captain as a brief look at his wristwatch snapped him out of the trance that he had been in. "Let's move up."

With the lieutenant's unnecessary help, I bundled up my few bits of kit, as he looked around with a look of equitable horror to my own just a few hours before.

"This war, it's funny isn't it? Machine guns used to cut men down in a more efficient fashion than before. But clubs and knives are still used in the same way as the middle ages. Very funny, don't you think?"

I gave a little smirk and a half-hearted shrug, "It seems like that's the only thing mankind has been good at for centuries…killing."

"Yes," he said, drawing out every letter as he raised his eyebrows, as if he was trying to recall his history lessons at Eton. "I suppose you're right. Goodbye, Corporal Ellis. I do hope to see you again soon."

"Likewise, Sir."

There were a few other muttered goodbyes, polite well-wishes to strangers that they had never met before, and more than likely would never reacquaint themselves with. As a group, we staggered through the communications trenches as Sergeant Hughes expertly navigated to our staging point on the frontline. He had either been here far longer than anyone else, or he had built the entire trench system himself, as he appeared to know where everything led, never stopping once to ask where we were amid all the repetitive and bland trenches.

Eventually we came to a dugout that was occupied by a handful of welcoming soldiers, as if they hadn't seen another man in a very long time. They took their light discipline extremely seriously, for the sake of their departing guests, making their eyes, the only part of their body that wasn't caked in mud, burn far brighter than a flare ever could. Their cheerful and optimistic expressions seemed to be exactly what I had needed, as I immediately felt buoyed by a sense of belonging, of familiarity at being back in the frontline, readying for action.

I caught a snippet of speech between Captain Arnold and the officer in charge of this stretch of the frontline.

"Your wire cutters have just gone over, Sir. Everything's gone off on time so far."

"Excellent, excellent."

The men who were keeping watch seemed fascinated by us, as we were some sort of species of elephant that they had never before seen nor heard of. They looked upon the Captain with particular admiration, before offering each of us a cigarette or a bite of chocolate.

I was suddenly filled with a warmness, and not just from the cigarette that dangled from between my lips. I had missed this feeling, the sense of being part of a group of men who cared about one another, to the point where they would die for the man next to them, even if they had only just met.

I had limited experience, but I missed the small amount of camaraderie between soldiers that I had been gifted when with five platoon, a couple of months gone by. I found myself longing to have the nerves in the pit of my stomach, the intestine tightening and the butterflies running rampant in my gut. Despite myself, I loved the feeling, being so near to death was what made a man feel alive.

My heart raced so fast that all the beats seemed to roll into one another, one long rumble in the centre of my chest that didn't seem like it had any desire to stop. As I breathed in slowly and carefully, trying to bring my heart back into line, I started to recall the names and faces of the men that I had lost before, the ones that I thought had disappeared into the abyss of my mind.

I saw Private Etwell, the broad-shouldered, god-like figure who had given me such a hard time and yet, taught me the most valuable lessons, as he stood shoulder to shoulder with the two jokers of our section; Sam Beattie and Doug Harris.

Sergeant Needs stood apart from the others and seemed far taller than I remembered, his stature still as perfect as ever to play in the centre of a rugby pitch. He held his chin high, as if he was looking down his nose at everything he saw, but in a majestic kind of way, not a condescending one.

I missed them and, as their spectral apparitions faded into the darkness of the dugout, I thought about their families; their wives, mothers, brothers, fathers and wondered if they had been informed about their deaths yet. I toyed with the idea that the army still had no idea who was dead or alive but eventually concluded, based on the amount of time that had passed, that they must have known by now. I felt eternally sorry for them.

The supernatural silence that wrapped the entire dugout in its embrace seemed only to incite more wonderful and fanciful imaginations in my mind, as I turned away from thinking about the past and looked to the near future.

I couldn't imagine what it was going to be like once we made it over there, but knew that there was a strong chance it was going to be a place where violence was jammed into every corner and crevice it could find, and the only way for me to combat that would be of a similar emotion swelling around in myself.

No one wanted to be the one to break the silence, if anyone held such a desire at all. There was no talking, no real means of communication other than an opened packet of cigarettes wafted beneath your nose. Even Earnshaw, the man who usually spoke with such garrulity, was spookily quiet, as if he had taken a lesson from the Captain on how to lock yourself within your own thoughts. He didn't even appear to be blinking.

I hoped that someone was keeping an eye on the time. There were men out there in No Man's Land already preparing the way for us. The very least we could do was to ensure that we left the frontline exactly when we were meant to.

I peered around in the darkness, trying to catch more than a darkened silhouette of the men that we were going to be leaving behind. I managed to catch a quick peek at one or two of them, as they lifted matches to their faces in order to light yet another cigarette. The army must be getting through millions of the things every single day.

Their faces carried young features, skin that seemed so soft on account of the fact that it hadn't had much chance to develop and become rougher. All of them were clean shaven, which didn't appear to be a result of choice, but because of Mother Nature's desires. As I looked at each of them, I could have sworn that their characteristics progressively got younger and younger, to the point that I thought if I continued to look, I might be confronted with a newborn baby.

Each one of them looked more nervous and twitchier than the last and I felt dismal on their behalf. This was probably the closest that they had got to the action since arriving on the frontline; the dark, mysterious figures pulling themselves into the night, the closest that they had got to this war.

They seemed naïve, and I wanted it to stay that way for as long as possible, just so long as they stayed switched on for the duration of the night, and that they remembered that there were friendlies out in No Man's Land tonight. It would be just my luck to get popped by a jumpy teenager gifted with one of His Majesty's rifles.

At the thought, I had to haul myself back into line. The possibility of being shot by one of my own men assumed as fact that I was going to make it that far anyway. Before then, I would have to negotiate No Man's Land, fight it out in an enemy trench, before withdrawing back over the desolate landscape once more. My hope that I was going to make it back was creeping up on me.

I was ignoring my own advice. I was ignoring the advice of my deceased Sergeant.

You're still holding onto your hope, you still think that you might make it out of here alive. But you can't think like that.

The words of Sergeant Needs seemed to trickle into my

consciousness once again, as it had done on so many other occasions previously, but this time, it sounded like my own voice uttering the words, not his gruff, father-like intonations.

It felt like George Needs had come back from the dead, just for a moment, to tell me off, to remind me of the faith that he for some reason had in me.

I pulled the flask from my breast pocket once again, trying to take a crafty swig from its mouthpiece.

GRHMN.

"You kept it?"

I looked across at Bob in the darkness, his deep brown eyes somehow glowing like they had become luminous in the dark.

"There's no way I'm going over there without it, mate. You want some?"

"No thank you," he said definitively. "One sip of that stuff and I'll be back in the latrines for another week." He began to chuckle quietly as he took in a mouthful of smoke, before the smile was wiped from his face completely. "Don't take too much of that though, will you? We might need some of the luck that it brings."

12

I DIDN'T KNOW what to have expected when I left the trenches, but for some reason my subconscious expectations were not met as I negotiated the British barbed wire. It was easy enough to drag our way through, there was strategic pauses in the wire to allow for such an excursion, but also to bottle neck the attacking forces if they ever did make the journey across to visit us.

The last time that I had been over the top of the frontline sandbags was on the last advance, the one where my entire platoon had been cut down within a matter of minutes and men had retreated with jaws hanging off, and with frightful injuries.

As I had hauled myself up the last few rungs of the trench ladder, held cautiously by a private who was perched in the trench on sentry duty, I half-wanted to see what I had seen before. I had seen great boggy shell holes, filled with all manner of creatures from rats and fleas to decomposing human bodies, and any other kind of mythical creatures.

The morning air had been filled with hisses and bangs, with artillery raining down on us like a child discarding a jar full of marbles. Men had been catapulted backwards by shrapnel and scythed down by machine gun bullets. I had paused for a moment and a section Corporal had taken molten steel to his chest and neck, saving me from feeling the effects of a detonating shell.

But, as I opened my eyes as I slithered past the wall of sandbags, I realised that my experience couldn't have been more different. All I could see was an incredible darkness, that wasn't so much pressing in, but forcing itself upon every inch of my body, as a liquid morphs around a solid object.

As a child, I used to be terrified of the darkness, paralysed by the prospect of a bogey man hiding in the shadows, or a murderer creeping around in the cavernous corners of my room. I had never come to a full appreciation of it, always wishing to some degree for the sun to come up and dispel my fears. It was only on that night, as we left the frontline, that I realised that now, I welcomed it, I embraced it.

Whereas before I had been petrified of the dark, it was now the light that made me feel like cowering.

I tortured my eyes as I laboured them to see in the dark, trying my utmost to pick out some of the other friendly faces that I knew were hiding out in the shell holes and debris that night. I thought for a moment that I caught sight of a skull-shaped shadow moving just above the ground, as one man defied orders to peek back and see if he could see us approaching. But, the more I looked at it, the closer that I moved my head towards it, I realised that it was nothing more than a mound of dirt, presumably chucked around by the forceful explosions of the artillery that gave the ground little respite.

As I continued to stare at the strange piece of dirt, I allowed my mind to wander ever so slightly, as I thought about the possibility that I had seen a fellow soldier out in No Man's Land. I wondered what his job had been, whether he had been one of the armed escorts for one of the preparatory teams, or maybe he had been part of the wire cutting section.

There was even the off chance that he wasn't part of this raid whatsoever. Maybe he was a wounded soldier from another raid or patrol. If he was, then maybe I would have been able to go over and find out, possibly even bring him back into our lines for treatment.

Before too long, the man was out of my mind, as I prayed that out of everyone taking part tonight, that the wire cutters had done a sterling job, and had the easiest work that they had ever come up against. A lot hinged on them.

If they had managed to clear the wire perfectly, with no disturbance from the Germans, then it could prove to be a much easier operation than I had first anticipated. If though, for example, a German sentry had been seen at the entry point, making it far harder for them to clear the wire stealthily, then there was a chance that we might never make it into the frontline itself.

I just hoped that it was the first scenario, and that they had done it flawlessly, so that I wasn't about to snag myself on a coil of barbed wire, ringing at the empty tin cans and other bells that they had fixed to their wire. All it would take would be the faintest brush of movement along one outstretched bit of wire and the entire raiding force would be lit up by an illuminating flare. That would be the end of that.

While I was mulling over every eventuality as to what might go wrong, I suddenly became increasingly concerned with our planned artillery bombardment. At the agreed time, the guns would open up, firing a huge amount of ordnance towards our flanks, to keep the inquisitive Hun in adjoining dugouts from racing to their comrades' assistance. That wasn't concerning me too much, as we were raiding the central sector of the line, which meant that the flanking bombardment would be a relatively safe distance away from us.

It was the shells that were due to drop just behind the frontline that had begun to scare me. They would fall around the parados of the trench, in the hope that as we made our final approach, the Boche would need to keep their heads down and thus miss our uninvited entry into their frontline.

I only hoped that the artillery commanders had fired a few practice shells earlier in the day, to make sure that they were falling exactly where they should, as I didn't much fancy being torn to shreds by a shell, not least by one of our own. There were so many factors that could affect the shell's path, from the dampness of the crate that they had been stored in, right up to the speed and direction of the wind, which I prayed they were keeping a beady eye on.

I felt Earnshaw tapping away at the sole of my boot, urging me to drag myself a few inches further forward to allow him to swing his legs off the top of the ladder and out into No Man's Land. I did as he had requested and watched him as he juddered his way towards me slowly, until he looked up at me with his thumb pointing to the sky.

Passing the boot tap further down the line, I waited until the column began to move off towards the German lines.

Up in the lead was Captain Arnold, with Sergeant Hughes half a metre further back and to his left side. Behind them was McKay and Bob in a similar pattern. Earnshaw and me bringing up the rear in the same manner as the others.

I made out a faint, low rustling as the fabric of our tunics slid almost noiselessly over the rough terrain, as I began to dig my elbows in to the mud like ice picks looking for some sort of a hold. I kept my bayonet in my right hand, the blade itself running the length of my forearm so I could avoid accidentally impaling my eyeballs on its fine point. My Webley appeared and disappeared in my vision as it stayed faithfully in my left palm.

I repeated myself over and over, keeping McKay's boot in my line of sight at all times. A few times I lost sight of it, and I felt like a lost child screaming at the top of his lungs for his mother, but I somehow resisted, until the point where I inevitably caught up with them.

We'd covered about twenty yards so far.

Only another three hundred or so to go.

∾

THE FLARE, that had carved a remorseless path up into the inky black night sky, hissed and spluttered as it fell to the ground, making inanimate objects suddenly come alive as we froze to the ground. We stopped dead in our tracks, planting our faces directly into the mud to hide ourselves as best as possible. For me, it was more so that I didn't have to look at the rounds that would shortly execute me.

As the flare died a solemn death, giving up its source of light with a depressive sigh, I pulled my head up. The Captain's head was already back up, flicking around in the darkness. I wondered for a moment if he had had his head down at all and thought maybe he had taken it upon himself to pinpoint our various waypoints early on, or maybe to scan ahead and see what opposition we might be met with.

My sockets burned brilliantly as the darkness began to take hold once again and I struggled to regain the ability to see in the dark, which was poor enough to begin with.

The Captain, even in the enshrouding darkness, was already thinking, imagining every possible outcome of where we were right now and thinking through his resolutions. He was straining so hard, I felt like I could see exactly what he was thinking.

Why send that flare up? Had they seen us? Maybe one of the other parties? Do they have their own party out?

He leant into Sergeant Hughes, who beckoned Bob up to his mouth, who in turn, did the same to me.

He spoke impossibly quietly and even though I could feel his lips moving along my ear, he sounded almost like a wind, a ghost.

"Stay alert. Could be an enemy patrol. Revolvers only if needed."

I repeated the message to Earnshaw who, surprisingly, only nodded in return. Maybe the reason he talked so much was to make up for the silence he had to adhere to out here.

I was suddenly very cold and wanted earnestly to begin moving again. The sweat that had formed up on my body as we had dragged ourselves through the mud began to chill on my skin, made worse still by the midnight breeze that caressed every hair on my body, bringing them to attention.

We began to move again, just as a wisp of cloud raced across and covered the stars from my gaze, giving them the appearance that they were in a game of hide and seek. I missed the comfort of the stars, their celestial warmth all I seemed to have as I made my way over the most desolate of landscapes. But, at the same time, the clouds were there to protect me, to bring a synthetic darkness over the landscape that was even blacker than the night itself.

The closer we edged to the German frontline, the more debris and resistance we came up against in our approach. I soon found myself rolling bodies out of my path, both German and British as they clogged up our chaotic route towards death. Some were in relatively good condition, as if they had stopped off only a few minutes ago for a sleep, apart from the stone-cold touch of their skin. Others were badly decomposed and felt frail, as if I could tear entire limbs off with nothing more than a swift tug.

I had no choice but to ignore them, and their smells, in order to keep up with the rest of the section and a slightly better chance at survival.

Suddenly, the pairs of boots in front of me began to disappear systematically, until Earnshaw was shoving me over to my left, forcing me into a water-filled shell hole.

Captain Arnold sat with his back up against one of the sloped sides of the shell hole, which looked suspiciously like it had been deepened with the aid of an entrenching tool or two. I could only wonder as to which side had been the ones to begin the digging.

"Machinegun number one will set up here. Our left-hand post as we head back to our lines. Try and use it as a marker if we get separated."

It felt good to be able to have some sort of reference point for when we headed back, and I began twisting and turning where I sat, to try and familiarise myself with the immediate area, giving myself the best chance at making it back in one piece.

"Don't pay too much attention to it, son," rasped Hughes, "terrain's likely to change by the time we head back out. Just remember its vague position."

I nodded, feeling foolish that I was trying to count the number of holes between here and the remnants of an old barn, that had been razed to nothing more than a few inches of bricks.

I felt Sergeant Hughes smirking in the darkness, my face blushing red under the layers of grease and grime that I had packed onto myself.

There was no chance for a break, no opportunity for some sort of breather, as we were soon slowly scrabbling our way back out of the hole and exposing ourselves to the elements once more.

My skin was soaked, and it felt as though every fibre of my itchy uniform was scratching at my body, to irritate me in any way that it could. We hadn't been crawling for all that long, twenty minutes maybe, and the prospect of having to stay in the same clothes for at least another couple of hours was one that filled me with misery. I had enjoyed my time in the frontline more than this.

I became breathless as we stopped again, doing everything within my power to prevent myself from wheezing and shrieking as I pulled in mouthful after mouthful of air. Now was not the time to make unnecessary noises; I could see the German wire.

What the Germans were doing in their trenches not to see or hear us approaching was beyond me, and could only suppose that their sentries had some sort of visual impairment. But I could hear the men in the dugout doing much the same that our men would do on a normal night; wandering up and down the trench, checking in with one another, making sure the sentries were okay for a smoke and generally trying to keep one another's morale up.

I found it odd, again, how normal these Germans were, how similar they were to our own troops. They were just men, like we were, sent here by invisible commanders to show an unholy amount of aggression towards an enemy who had really done no wrong to us. I was beginning to show a compassion for the men that I would soon be asked to kill.

All we could do now was lie here in wait. I knew that the Captain would be checking his wristwatch impatiently every ten seconds or so, waiting until he knew that everyone else would be in position, then all we would be waiting for would be that first artillery shell.

I wondered if the wire cutters had managed to hear the Germans with the same clarity that I now could, or whether, on account of the hour, their voices carried far more powerfully. I concluded that they must have heard them talking, possibly using their own noise against them, to be able to snip away at the wire that would allow us free entry.

It was a grave mistake on the Germans' part and one that I believed meant that they should lose the entire war.

Just as I felt my body beginning to be enveloped in the ever-pressing chill, I thought I heard a noise. Already being completely still, I froze everything else that was moving; my heart, my lungs, my blood and listened.

Then it was there again, far in the distance, but noticeable if you were listening specifically for it.

Thumm. Thumm. Thumm.

13

THE ARTILLERY SHELLS had barely uttered their first syllable announcing their arrival and Captain Arnold was already on his feet and leaping down into the German dugout. He jumped with such a vigour and athleticism that I thought he had miscalculated and had ended up on the far side of the trench.

I had no time to calculate whether the Captain's jumps were misjudged or not, as within seconds, it was my turn to leap down into the dugout and begin to assess what was going on.

I had half a second to myself before I was pulled from my frozen state, by which time most of the raiders already had a subject at their fingertips and were beginning to beat them black and blue. The Germans seemed totally unwilling to put up anything that resembled a fight, instead opting to simply take a jolly good beating from their enemy.

The raiders had jumped upon them with such short notice that the Germans barely had time to bring their weapons to bear, meaning they were simply knocked to the ground as twelve stone of purebred British soldier crumpled down on top of them.

The Captain already had one man down to the ground, a swift, elegant and jaw-breaking punch landed on the underside of his chin, which sent teeth flying upwards and the German in the opposite direction. He now writhed around on the floor in agony, clutching at his mouth which was filling up nicely with blood, completely out of the action for the time being.

Sergeant Hughes had become a man possessed and had clubbed a man over the head with his nail-embedded truncheon, splitting the man's skull open before moving on to anyone else who seemed to want to put up a fight.

Even McKay was getting stuck in, shouting in a coarse German tone to his subject as he landed blow after blow to the German's chest. I could see now why he had been called the physical persuader. Within seconds the German had no option but to do what the broad shouldered and threatening McKay told him to do, and I was certain that I had just identified our first prisoner of the night.

A cutthroat roar suddenly exploded in my ear drums, and I turned just in time to watch a man, presumably an enemy soldier, charge towards me, his peak-less forage cap lolling over to one side, as if he had just been woken up from his sleep.

It seemed like he had, as he offered up no sort of resistance and graciously ran straight into my oncoming fist, which knocked him over as if the rug had been pulled from under his feet. He cannoned backwards for half a second and I thought I might have killed the man with a single hit for a fleeting moment. He lay on the floor unconscious and

I had no time nor inclination to check and see if he was okay.

"Tie him to me! Tie him to me!" screamed McKay, as he launched a length of rope in my direction. Under his other arm he more or less carried his prisoner in a headlock, the poor young man drifting in and out of consciousness and leaking blood everywhere.

I did as McKay told me, securing the prisoner around his waist before giving a sharp tug on the rope to double check its security.

"You're good to go, McKay! He's all yours!"

The artillery was making an almighty racket, the great whooshes sounding like an express train as it shot its way through a station. The ground shook with each explosion sending towers of dirt and rubble in every direction, making it feel like it was raining mud in the trench.

McKay began to growl at his prisoner, as he staggered around trying to stop McKay from having an excuse to put a bullet in his skull. But it seemed that McKay was talking to him most compassionately, soothingly almost, as if he was talking to a friend and not an enemy.

"What now, McKay? Where do I go from here?"

The others had begun to scrabble around for papers, or put the finishing touches to the black and blue make up that they were applying to the remaining few conscious stragglers.

The Captain, above another volley of three shell bursts, interrupted his reply. "Take Earnshaw! Move to the next dugout. There's a machine gun there. Try and disable it!"

Before he could finish, Earnshaw was already making his way over to me, revolver up and ready. I assumed the same position and began to creep around the corner, as if reducing my noise might help me in my next phase of operations.

As I approached the corner, I thought I caught a flash of movement on the other side of the wall. I wasn't able to give it a second thought as in the next moment, a German bolted around the corner and came face to face with me.

He seemed totally unprepared for what was about to happen next. He had no weapon from what I could see, nothing on his head and it appeared like all he was doing was coming round into the next dugout to warn them of the trench raid that was going on further down the line.

I swung my elbow up and round, catching him on the crook of his nose with my best impression of a flailing chicken wing. He staggered for a moment, but was soon aware as to what was happening, as if my blow had done nothing other than wake him up.

He flung a fist towards me wildly, slamming into my cheekbone with an almighty explosion of pain. My vision in my right eye suddenly became hazy and I felt the side of my face burn as blood rushed to the source of the pain.

I stumbled backwards in response, as the now-snarling German, grinning at the realisation that his opponent was already on the ropes, came at me for a second pass.

The second blow caught me on the temple, and I felt an eruption of pain, even greater than the last, as it seemed like a tidal wave of blood and pain washed through the frontal lobe of my brain. Immediately, I was fighting off a headache as well as the fighting German, who picked up an entrenching tool that was leaning against the wall of the trench and came at me with it.

He raised the weapon high above his head, bringing it down with a grunt and swish as it carved its way through the air. Instinctively, I pulled my right arm in a defensive block instantly feeling it shatter as it gave way under the pressure of his might.

I bellowed in pain as I realised the German too was screaming, probably more out of frustration that he hadn't been able to put me down yet. I waited for him to lift the tool above his own height for a second time, knowing that I had to put this to bed before he smashed all of my limbs to pieces.

As the weapon went up, he left his torso completely exposed, and I threw myself at him as hard as I could, hoping that my momentum would carry me forward and exaggerate the blow that he would feel.

I slammed into him, my left arm out at a strange angle, and I felt the hilt of the bayonet dig into my ribs as the business end was forced into his chest. I felt the bayonet chip away at organs and bone, but surprisingly little resistance was put up by the German's internals, and soon the full length of the bayonet had been plunged into his skin.

I had been hoping that the pain might make him immediately sink to his knees, dropping the weapon harmlessly to the floor. But I was mistaken.

The German fought on heroically, bellowing out in pain like the wounded Beowulf, bringing the tool down hard on the back of my neck, making me crumple into a heap like a house of playing cards.

The entrenching tool fell down beside me as I fell, but I still clung onto the bayonet, dragging it downwards with me as I came down. It must have ripped through the German's skin in the most awful of ways, as he soon sunk to his knees in agony.

"Nice fighting, Ellis. Now get up."

Earnshaw had finally made his way over to me, in time to watch me scrabble around, pulling the bayonet from my victim.

As he strolled past, as if what he had just witnessed was no more exciting than watching a flower grow, he took his own bayonet, and sunk it straight into the German's throat, practically pinning the poor man to the floor.

"Come on, let's get a move on. Not long to go," he said, as the German's gurgles slowly faded into nothing, blood gushing from the open wound in his neck, coating both mine and Earnshaw's boots.

He peeked his head around the corner, trying to look down the length of the next dugout.

"There's a few in there. About five I reckon. Don't look like they really know what to do. Machinegun is about halfway down. You got any jam tins?" He asked me, as he hurriedly began pulling out a packet of cigarettes and forced one into my mouth.

"Just the one."

"Good, I've got two. You take one of mine, we'll fight our way down the dugout and you'll place both under the machine gun, light them then we fall back. Use your revolver for this one, I reckon we can gun them down before they can even fire back at us." He looked back at me with a wink, "And don't miss."

He lit the cigarette that hung from his mouth, before using it to light mine for me. I clamped my mouth around it tightly, as there was a very strong possibility that this would be the most important cigarette of my life. It was a good job that I had picked up on the habit.

I swung my satchel round, so that it was resting in the

small of my back, in case we were fired upon and I went up in a cloud of explosives, spent casings and rusty nails. My bayonet was slid up my sleeve and held in place by my revolver wielding hand.

Carefully, Harry took his cigarette from his mouth and gently pressed it on the end of the fuse that protruded from the top of the tin. He watched it as it fizzed and hissed, burning slowly towards the can and the inevitable explosion. As soon as it had burned through to the desired point, his body jolted suddenly as he flew from the cover of the trench wall.

He lobbed the can as far as he could, and I struggled to see where it had actually landed. Before it exploded, he was already trying his best to pick off the soldiers who were airily wandering around the trench, not really knowing which direction to turn or run to.

Earnshaw managed three rounds before the jam tin exploded, a fireball suddenly erupting at the far end, as I heard the multiple pieces of shrapnel barrel through the air. I saw two men go down, neither of them dead but wounded enough to be distracted from our presence.

There were three others still standing, who quickly flicked their rifles up and were already sending rounds our way. It must have been really dark for them, as their rounds were hitting everywhere around the trench apart from us.

It was either that or we had some sort of divine shield wrapped around us, as two bodies, side by side, filled up the width of the trench meaning it was almost impossible to miss.

They paid for their mistakes, as I thundered two rounds into one enemy soldier, and Earnshaw managed to bury one in another. The final one fired off one more wayward round, before scarpering into the next dugout, presumably where he would meet the same fate as his comrades.

"The machine gun, quickly!" strained Earnshaw, his voice faltering and far from its normal triumphant self. I glanced across at him.

He clutched at his side, as if he had a stitch, but the unmistakeable pigment of blood seeping through his fingers was obvious, even in the darkness.

"The gun, Ellis!"

I did as he told me, dabbing my cigarette on the two fuses which now brushed the underside of the machinegun barrel tenderly.

They crackled away, my immediate attention thrust towards Harry as he grunted and grimaced in the darkness.

"Come on, let's get you out of here," I wheezed as I pulled his good side towards my shoulder. I dragged him backwards towards the rest of our friends, just about disappearing behind the cover of the trench wall corner, as the jam tins exploded, the sound of metal becoming deformed like an angelic choir to our ears.

∾

A GUNSHOT FLASHED AWAY at the far end of the dugout as we both appeared around the corner.

"Damn! He got away! I missed!" Sergeant Hughes reeled from his latest mishap, before turning and seeing one silhouette that had four arms and four limbs. "How bad is he hit?" he shouted across at me, as I realised that his calm and gentle persona had completely melted away.

"Took a ricochet off the side of the wall, I think. The bleeding's pretty bad, but not as bad as he's making out."

"Lost all sympathy for me already have you?" his yellowing teeth grinned up at me.

"Right then gents. Let's begin to get this wrapped up, then shall we? We have three minutes left before the artillery redirects their fire. Plus, we'll probably need a little extra time to get out now."

Captain Arnold almost sounded disappointed at Earnshaw for getting himself wounded, appearing to much prefer the option that he was killed.

Hughes had begun to tie a second prisoner around Bob's waist and I stared at his petrified little eyes as they glared back at me. I wondered who was feeling more scared at the moment; the German or Bob?

I gave him a quick nod, which seemed to give him an unphysical slapping, as his face changed to one of determination and fearlessness.

Four shells burst just above the back of the trench, making us all instinctively duck down. The Captain had to repeat what he had just said.

"Those with jam tins, lob them into the corners of the dugouts. Let's get out of here."

McKay had been standing at the foot of the trench ladder, staring at it and bouncing around as if he had a genuine itch to leave the frontline before anyone else. He tugged at his prisoner, pointing his revolver in his face and then up and towards No Man's Land. The prisoner got the idea.

As he placed his first hand on the ladder, the fuses began to hiss again as they were lit and thrown into the darkest corners of the trench, one final kick in the teeth for the Germans who would now have to rebuild part of their lines.

"Earnshaw, you next. We'll patch you up when we can. You'll have to suck it up for now."

An involuntary "Sarge," passed over his lips, as he was pushed up the ladder by his buttocks, and gruffly yanked up by his armpits, as McKay reappeared at the top of the ladder.

Finally, my eyes peeled so far apart that it felt like I had forgotten how to blink, it was my turn to head up the ladder. The Captain hot on my heels behind.

As I got to the top of the ladder, I heard the unmistakeable hiss of another jam tin beginning to sizzle, and turned just in time to watch the Captain throw it towards the centre of the trench, from where he had managed to bundle up most of the maps and papers that were now stuffed in his satchel.

"Go, go!" he hissed at me as he galloped up the ladder.

With that, each one of us was back out in No Man's Land, with two passengers along for the ride.

14

I SCRABBLED around in the mud, trying to negotiate the small patch of land between the top of the parapet and the cut wire. The renewed dampness to my skin irritated me even further, and I could feel my skin beginning to redden in patches in the worst hit areas.

The sweat that was rolling down my face was so profuse, that I was certain within minutes all the burnt cork and grease that I had packed on, would soon be completely washed away and I would be nothing more than a glowing target in the dark landscape.

I suddenly jolted to a halt as I pulled my way in between the barbed wire. Clearly, the incision into the wire had not been as clean as I had hoped, as a coil had wrapped its way around my lower leg, its talons biting into my left knee as I wriggled.

The cans on the other coils of wire began to tinkle, almost inaudible above the artillery that was almost certainly increasing in intensity now. I was trapped, and the more I tried to pull myself free or wriggle my way out, the more in pain and entangled I became.

"We don't have time for this, Ellis," the Captain grunted as he slid his way up next to me.

"Sorry, Sir. I didn't see it."

"Doesn't matter, hold still."

We had nothing to cut the wire with, nothing to protect our hands in case we needed to grip it suddenly, which is what made it all the more surprising when the Captain clamped his hand around the coil, without so much of a grimace.

Carefully and most gently, he began to peel the claws of the wire out from my leg, before unwinding the coil and pushing me through.

The pain grew exponentially as I began to drag myself clear of the wire, before stopping to double check that the same didn't happen to the Captain. Of course, it wouldn't, he was a far better soldier than I was.

"Thanks, Sir."

"Don't mention it. Keep moving, catch up with the others."

No sooner had I turned back to face front again, then great fountains of dirt began to spring up everywhere, like a natural spring. The ground trembled soon afterwards, further shaking dirt and mud all over my body, soaking up the dribble of blood that was now rolling down the front of my shin.

Pulling myself up into a crawling position, I scrabbled my way forwards, trying to make more ground than when I was on my belly, not fully trusting the accuracy of the artillery's rounds. I felt the Captain do the same, until we were at a safe enough distance to drop back down to our bellies.

We caught up with the others, who were lying on the floor in some sort of diamond pattern, waiting for the final two languishers to catch up with them.

"I think we're at a safe enough distance to stand now, Sir," whispered Hughes, "I think we did enough damage to put them off from shooting at us."

"I don't know about that second bit Sergeant. But yes, agreed. We need to prioritise speed now, especially with our friends in tow."

McKay was struggling with his prisoner, tugging at the rope as he tried to scrabble back towards the German frontline.

"You okay, McKay?"

"Yes Sir, I don't think this one likes staying still for very long, he's very fidgety."

"Let's get a move on then, shall we?"

Bob's prisoner seemed to be behaving far better than McKay's and as we began to move off again, it seemed like they had bonded in some way.

We waddled along at first, keeping our heads as low as possible but moving infinitely faster, before we were able to stretch our legs out slightly and jog in a stooped sprint. It was risky, even in the dark, but we wanted to make it back to the frontline before the Germans sprayed the entire area with bullets and bombs.

I was feeling good, apart from the dull ache in my knee from where the barbed wire had bitten me. But we had done what we had gone to do; we had raided the German trench and taken them by complete surprise, we had destroyed key bits of equipment and also left with two prisoners, all without a single fatality.

Earnshaw was moving slower than the rest of us, but he was still moving, as was I, which filled me with a joy that would spread itself across my face just as soon as I was definitely safe. There was still a long way to go yet.

I wondered how the other raiding parties on both our flanks were faring, and if they had left with a couple of prisoners each as well. If that was the case, then we would end up with six enemy prisoners, which was surely more than enough to identify the regiments that we were facing. Maybe even one of them was an officer, who would be able to tell us far more than the average man that was dug in there. I was wishfully hoping.

The ear-splitting bangs, as shell after shell began to throw itself into the ground, began to put an immense pressure on my eardrums. I felt the pressure begin to grow to the point where I thought I would not be able to bear it any longer and either my eardrums would burst, or my entire head would explode.

The volume of shells had increased greatly in the last twenty seconds or so, to the point where I thought that maybe the Germans were responding with a salvo of their own. I began trying to count the dull thuds, numbed slightly by my bleeding ears, but I quickly lost count after twenty, as trying to distinguish whether there was one shell or five became completely impossible.

As if all the unbearable noises were in cahoots with one another, a machine gun suddenly began spouting rounds out of its barrel, directly above my left ear, which sent me clutching for it immediately as if it was being severed off.

I turned my head away from the gun, whereupon I could see the other machine gun, perhaps a hundred yards away, spitting rounds out in much the same fashion and blinking great flashes of light around the surrounding area.

The guns would converge on one another before too long, creating a lethal killing field for anything and anyone who dared to lift themselves above the parapet. I thought the likelihood of them actually popping anyone tonight would be rather minimal; if the Germans had any sense at all they would bury themselves at the bottom of their dugouts and ride the storm out.

I supposed that the enemy weren't being as bright as they perhaps could have been, as I suddenly felt rounds zipping past my head and burrowing their way into the soft soil all around me. A gun from somewhere in the German frontline must have been opening up, aiming at the only thing that they could see; the flashing muzzle of machine guns out in No Man's Land.

"Move away from the guns! Get away from them!" I couldn't work out who was screaming, but we all did as we were told, quite gladly. There was no point in being close to the only thing in No Man's Land that was drawing any kind of fire.

The constant rattle of the machine guns was suddenly interrupted by what sounded like an inverted whistle, as if someone was trying to suck in air rather than expel it. The next thing I felt was the incredible pressure wave that rippled across my whole body, and I felt all of my organs suddenly wriggle around as they were pulverised by an invisible wall.

I went blind for a moment as shards of dried mud settled on my eyeballs, causing me to blink furiously so that I could see again. The pain subsided enough for me to watch the final few clouds of dirt disappear in the darkness, and I scrabbled to the nearest shell hole that I could find, to recoup and work out what had happened.

I found myself coughing and spluttering in the bottom of a crater that was knee-high with water, the dirt and grime floating around in it seeping nicely into the ripped flesh of my knee.

The Captain began to get his breath back, "You okay?"

"I'm fine, just got dirt in my eyes."

"Good, we'll wait here a second. I didn't see what happened to the others."

There was silence for a moment, as if the machine guns had stopped and the artillery had simply given up. In the short gap of peace, I couldn't hear any moans or screams, that so often accompanied a group who had been hit by an artillery shell.

Before long, the noises were back, the machine gun was hammering away at the German's sandbags and the artillery was still howling overhead like an overexcited child. It didn't seem that the Germans were firing back just yet.

"Must have just been a duff round," I exclaimed as I looked across at the Captain.

"Yep. We need to get a move on then, hopefully we'll catch up with the others."

I caught sight of Earnshaw and waddled my way over to him.

"Where did you get to?" he hollered, scanning just behind our backs as if he was looking for someone else.

"Got knocked off our feet. We're okay to carry on though."

"Okay, wh—"

One of the machine guns suddenly stopped firing and a shrill screaming took over in its place. Everyone fell on their faces and hugged the ground. One of the gunners must have been hit by a lucky German round.

I suddenly felt very guilty and wondered if I had in fact destroyed the machinegun that I had tried to blow up, or simply dented a small bit of metal allowing it to continue firing on us.

"Keep moving," hissed the Captain from the rear of our column, as we began to carry on our withdrawal on our bellies, snaking our way to the British frontline. We couldn't have too much further to go now.

Comfortingly, the machine gun sparked back up again, this time with the underlying soundtrack of a mortally wounded man added into the mix. It was difficult not to want to turn back and pull the man out of there, but that wasn't our task to fulfil.

Besides, I was hampered by my own pain, the one that was shooting up and down my leg like a pendulum, especially after I had dropped into the scummy water of the crater a few minutes before. The throbbing in my forearm and head, courtesy of the now deceased German, was also doing nothing to assist me. The pain, although obvious, was far less debilitating than the last time I had ventured out into No Man's Land and an even greater success.

I was returning with every man that I had set out with, compared to just one companion last time. I felt good, buoyed by the success of this operation and for half a second, I looked forward to going out with these boys again sometime soon.

I strained my eyes until I could see Bob and his prisoner, waddling their way around in much the same manner as I was. I wondered if Bob was feeling the same as me, the only other person in the world who could vaguely understand the pain that I had gone through at the loss of an almost entire platoon.

Touching my breast pocket, to check that it hadn't fallen out in the German trench or anywhere else for that matter, I wondered if Sergeant Needs would have been proud of his two youngest recruits. We had been the newbies of his section, the ones that he had to keep an eye on and gee up in preparation for going over the top.

Now, here we were, dragging two prisoners back to our lines in what could only have been described as an overwhelming success.

The several pairs of feet up ahead of me suddenly stopped, congregating once more by lying flat on our bellies. Bob was really getting into the prison guard routine, pushing his captive's head down until it was pressed into the dirt, the German seemingly intent on trying to get his head blown off instead of coming into our lines.

The Captain slid his way expertly to the front of our column and I could just about hear him as he whispered to his Sergeant.

"Okay then, Nicholas. Go and warn them we're coming back in."

Hughes acknowledged the Captain by beginning to slide his way towards the barbed wire that I could see just ahead of us. For a horrible moment I thought that, in all the chaos and confusion, that we had somehow become lost and had crawled straight back to the German line, but soon tried to put the image from my mind.

I willed the young lads in the trench to take a half second pause before squeezing the trigger, in case they accidentally slotted Sergeant Hughes in a case of mistaken identity. Fortunately, there were no gunshots, no sounds of moaning as he was unexpectedly bayoneted and no shouts of German to be heard.

Instead, just a lone, soft voice appeared in the gloom, the one that we had all been waiting for, the one that meant we were safe.

"Okay, chaps. Come on in."

15

"Well done, Ellis."

"Thank you, Sir."

"You did well. Harry told me that you took out that machinegun nicely. Good job, that'll take the gun off the line for a few days."

"Hope so, Sir."

The Captain gave me a gentle whack on the shoulder as he padded his way over to his next soldier, getting ready to congratulate them on a job well done also. I watched as everyone went about congratulating one another, as if we had just won the FA cup final.

"Andrew," gasped Bob as he made his way over to me, cigarette already in his mouth, "how did you find it? All go okay?"

"Yeah," I replied, breathlessly, "it went well. In fact, I think I kind of enjoyed it. What about you? Any hitches?"

"None whatsoever," he said, pushing a smoke into my mouth and lighting it. "I even made a friend."

He flicked his head in the general direction of his prisoner, who was now under the watchful eye of Sergeant Hughes, who was giving him a cigarette to help calm him down. We weren't the monsters that his generals would have them believe.

"Where's the other one?"

"What?"

"The other prisoner," I said, taking in a nice long drag, "we had two."

"Oh…yeah, er I suppose they'll be along in a minute or two. Once the hubbub dies down, I reckon."

I looked around at all the jovial, grinning faces, the light restrictions slightly lifted now that we had done what we had set out to do. I could see toothless smiles and young ones, nervous and flamboyant ones. Everyone seemed to be having a great time.

Earnshaw was already being patched up by one of the medics who had been awaiting our arrival, as he heroically told his story of how he had really stuck it to the enemy. The young infantrymen all around us were totally engrossed. I was too, he managed to make the whole affair sound rather grandiose.

He caught my disapproving eye and winked. I wondered how many more layers would be added on by the time we made it back to Le Plantin and where all the local girls were.

A couple of Military Police NCOs came around the corner, immediately subduing the party atmosphere in the frontline trench. Captain Arnold immediately made himself known to the three men who had appeared to take the prisoners away. Bob looked genuinely upset at the loss of his new friend.

The infantrymen went back to their stations, some of

them continuing the letters that they had started earlier in the day or staring at the photos that were tucked in their pockets. Whatever they did, each one of them seemed relieved that the action for tonight seemed to be over, and that they could get back to a sense of normality for the rest of the day.

"Where's the—"

This time the Captain was interrupted, by a sudden burst of machine gun fire, that seemed to echo far louder than anything else out in No Man's Land.

"Where's the other prisoner? We left with two. Where is he?" He looked around at each of us accusingly for a moment, before having to compose himself as he faced the police officers irritatingly awaiting his response.

They looked shifty, their eyes darting to the skies every now and then as if expecting a large barrage to suddenly drop on our position. I hadn't made my acquaintances with these men before and had never seen them in the frontline to date, which made me assume that they were normally behind the lines, doing whatever they did on a day to day basis.

"I'm sorry gentlemen, the other one must have got away. Maybe he was picked off in No Man's Land. Still, we fulfilled our quota."

The NCOs saluted the Captain, offering up no kind of argument or counter measure to the missing prisoner. They seemed downright excited at the prospect of getting out of the frontline. Within seconds, they were leading their prisoner away, manhandling far more roughly than Bob had done when we had been under fire. I hoped that they would continue to give him some cigarettes at the very least.

"You lot. Over here." The Captain seemed furious, as if each one of us had been personally responsible for the missing prisoner. It seemed he didn't like to made a fool out of, especially in front of the military police and the young infantrymen.

"Right," he accused, looking at each one of us in turn, as if he was trying to read our eyes before asking the inevitable question. "Where's the other one? Why did we leave with two and only end up with one? How can we possibly be a prisoner down?"

"Not just a prisoner, Sir," spoke Hughes, obviously far more comfortable with the Captain than any of us others. "We're a man down too."

The Captain flicked his head over towards Hughes, simultaneously checking that none of his admiring infantry were listening in. They weren't; they were far too preoccupied with writing letters home to their mothers and fathers. They didn't care what we were up to.

"What?" his voice was abrupt and brusque, his lips suddenly tightening as his jaw clenched firmly.

"McKay...Sir. He's not here, didn't come back in."

"How have we only just noticed this?"

"He was falling behind, Sir. Then you got hit by that shell. We thought he had fallen in with you."

"And he had the other prisoner?"

"Yes, Sir," I croaked, "I tied him to McKay."

No one said anything, but instead let the Captain try to work things out in his own mind, as he so often did. Except, this time, he didn't do it independently and quietly, but loudly, muttering his different hypothesis to himself at the speed of sound. His arms flapped around as he ran his fingers through his hair and then down his neck. He was flustered, genuinely worried, and it didn't suit him in the slightest.

"We could head back out there, Sir. See if we can find him?" Earnshaw was raring to go, despite the great dressing that had been tied to his side to stem the bleeding for a while.

There was a general mutter around the group that showed there was an agreement to the proposal.

Hughes sat quite firmly on the other side of the fence, "No chance. He most likely got pinged by that shell or maybe their guns that had opened up. There's no way we're risking all of your lives for the sake of a prisoner and McKay. No way."

"But, sarge," I said, bewildered at myself for wanting to head back out there when I had the opportunity to head straight back to the *Café de fleurs*. "He was directly in front of me. I could see his feet for most of it. If he had got pinged, I would have heard something, if not from McKay, then from his prisoner. Surely?"

"Maybe he just got disorientated," added Bob. "He could just be lost."

"And no one else saw him go down?" the Captain broke his silence as he massaged his chin.

"Well, if he didn't get hit when we were all out there, there's a good chance he's been pinged since. There was a lot of concentrated fire out there," Hughes began to rub away at the wrinkles on his forehead, which seemed to be moving far more than his lips at the moment.

The Captain sighed no less than three times, as he rolled his eyes and stroked his chin for a few moments more. He had always struck me as a decisive and certain individual, never taking any longer than was strictly necessary to come to a decision. But this time, he was taking longer than usual. Too long.

He was genuinely conflicted about the possibility of losing one man, even if that meant sacrificing the other four just to try and get him back.

Observing the strife and turmoil that his Captain and friend was going through, Hughes helped the decision along.

"Sir, if we're going to go, we'll have to go sooner, rather than later. We only have a very small window in which to affect a proper search. The machine guns will be withdrawing soon, and our oppressive artillery will cease. We need to be out there and preferably on our way back before that happens, or we'll be stuffed."

"He may only be a few yards from the barbed wire, Sir. We won't know until we've double checked," Earnshaw chipped in from the crate that he was perched on.

He took a second or two longer to think things through, a prolonged rattle of machine gun fire sounding as if to reiterate the point about the protection they could offer. He took a quick glance over his shoulder again, peering at the young infantrymen that were still sitting a way away, doing their own thing.

"Okay," he said eventually, "we'll go back out and have a quick scoot around. If we haven't found him by the time the machineguns stop, we'll head back. We'll have to conclude that he got hit somewhere along the way."

He rubbed his eyes for a second or two, as we waited patiently for what he might say next.

"I won't make anyone go if you don't want to. This is strictly voluntary."

We each waited for a few seconds, giving one another

time to think about their commitment to the team and McKay.

Nothing went through my mind for a while, but then suddenly, something that Earnshaw had told me the day before struck me.

The Captain doesn't like half-hearted volunteers.

"I'll go, Sir," I said, as forcefully and as upbeat as I could possibly muster. The Captain gave me a quick nod in return.

"Me too, Sir."

Bob was in.

"And me, Captain."

So was Earnshaw.

"Well, I guess we're all coming then Captain."

"Okay, thank you everyone. But Earnshaw, I don't think you should come with us—"

"But, Sir—"

"No, I've made my decision. You're hurt. You would only slow us down and we need to be as quick as possible."

Earnshaw dejectedly accepted the Captain's blunt statement, he knew that he was right.

"Can you walk, Harry?"

"Yes, Sir."

"Well then, you can be of some use. Can you source us four rifles from one of your friends behind the lines and get them sent up here ASAP? We're going to be requisitioning some from these boy soldiers here."

Earnshaw's face suddenly lit up. I could tell he already knew exactly who he was going to go to.

"The rest of you, grab a rifle from one of these boys. And as many rounds as they can give you."

The Captain's personality change from indecisive, troubled leader to all out battle commander was in full force, as he issued instructions to everyone in the dugout, which seemed to annoy the young lieutenant in charge of the platoon.

"I want everyone up on the fire step. No exceptions, even you lot without the rifles. Keep your eyes peeled and make sure that machinegun is ready. We've got a man out there and there's a very strong possibility that we'll have a Boche patrol hot on our heels when we come back in. If we do, open fire immediately, even if that means dropping one of us to get a clear shot at the Hun. Understood?"

My gut tightened once again at the thought of being chopped down by one of our own bullets. I felt my jaw tighten as I thought about the possibility that, even if the Germans weren't on our tails, that these boys were now so riled up that they were going to shoot at anything that moved.

But I had volunteered, there was no going back on my word now. McKay was out there, possibly wounded, potentially disorientated and I hoped sincerely that he would have volunteered to do exactly the same if it had been me that had been left out there.

The Captain snatched a Very light from an opened crate and stuffed it down the side of his trousers, after waving it about a bit.

"I'm taking this. When you see it, it means that we're about to come back in. We'll move as soon as the light fades. Understood? I need you all to acknowledge that."

They did as they were told, quite fearful of the man who had suddenly gone from triumphant leader to aggressive dictator.

"You three ready?" he said turning to us.

We each checked our rifles had a round ready in the breech, before rocking the safety catches off.

As a trio, we nodded.

For the second time that night, we headed back into No Man's Land.

16

We stayed as low as we possibly could but moved much faster and significantly louder than the last time we had been out here. I couldn't quite believe that I was once again heading towards the German frontline, particularly as it had been completely voluntary.

But there had been something about McKay, something that had drawn me to him and made me feel quite sorry for him from the moment that I had met him. Maybe it had been the way that he quite clearly could fight for himself physically, but emotionally he was shot to pieces.

The Captain could see it too, I was quite sure of that and began to recall all the times that everyone else had defended McKay as much as they possibly could. He was the one that everyone felt like they needed to look out for, his mind in bits after everything that he had experienced.

"Stay low," whispered Hughes from the front of our column, as we convened behind a pile of rubble and flattened ourselves out on the ground. He began to slide forwards slowly, his rifle wiggling from side to side like they were a set of handlebars on a bicycle.

I wondered how we were going to conduct the search the closer we got to the German lines. We didn't have long left before the artillery and machineguns ceased, which meant that they would have their sentries and lookouts back up in no time.

The closer we got to the frontline, the more craters we would have to check in, which meant it was going to be almost impossible for us to stay undetected.

"Spread out slightly," rasped the Captain, "just in case."

I left it a few seconds before following on behind him, like I knew Bob would do in the next few seconds with me.

Quite abruptly, and as if someone had flicked off a switch, the machine guns fell silent. We all stopped for a second, hoping more than anything that it was just so that they could reload rather than them disengaging. But, I knew that, if I was to look at the Captain's wristwatch, it would tell me that it was fifteen minutes past one in the morning and that we were now without our oppressive fire.

I imagined the gunners packing up their kit, before withdrawing silently in the knowledge that they would be back in British lines in the next few minutes. I prayed that they were decent blokes, maybe even volunteering to give us more covering fire as we moved about the craters. But I knew it was a futile thought, no one in their right mind would allow them to come back out, especially as the chances of hitting their own men would increase tenfold.

The artillery was doing a decent enough job of keeping the enemy's heads down, but before long that too would stop and we would be left alone, to fend for ourselves against a raging enemy that had just had so many of its compatriots murdered.

We drew closer to the enemy trench and the thought occurred to me that we must have passed McKay by now, whether he was alive or dead. He had still been a part of the column when the shell fell short, forcing both the Captain and me into a crater, which meant he was only around one hundred or so yards away from the British lines. We were now at least two hundred into No Man's Land.

We were going to need to find him and fast, before the Germans began to retaliate with their own artillery and machineguns, otherwise we would all be killed within the next few minutes. We would have to turn back to keep searching for him.

Suddenly, with a depressing, fleeting thud, the final three artillery shells slammed into the enemy lines. Direct hits.

Then, as the dust began to waft towards us, there was silence. I drank it in and almost began to enjoy it until I heard the swishing of fabric moving around on the ground as we were all pulled down into a large shell hole.

We huddled together, sitting shoulder to shoulder so that we could hear one another.

"In all honesty chaps, I think we should stop," Hughes' face was one of dejection and misery. "I just can't see how we're going to find him. The situation is too volatile."

"I would be inclined to agree with the Sergeant," Bob said, with an equal helping of despondency.

The Captain looked over at me, as if he was just waiting for someone to at least fight for the other side.

"I think we should head back. I don't think he would have been this close to their lines. I say we continue the search closer to our own lines."

"He must have taken a hit on the way back in," Hughes began to reason, "Maybe his German got pinged and dragged him down. Who knows. Either way, I think unfortunately Fritz hasn't survived."

"I think we should go on."

"Sir, with all due respect, it's far too risky now. You'll get yourself killed."

He took a few more moments in his own thoughts, for which we all stayed silent. We had learned quite quickly that he didn't respond to any kind of communication when he was like this, not even if he was being fired upon.

I trusted him to make the right decision, but I was unsure over whether that decision would take me one step closer to having bullets ripping through my flesh. I wished that I had never volunteered to start with.

The silence was extraordinary, and I began to get some feeling back into my ears as they recuperated. The blood that was pumped into them was excruciating, but it filled me with pleasure that within a few minutes, it was likely my hearing would be back up to full strength. Even if that did mean I heard the rifle cracks that killed me.

"I've made my decision," he eventually whispered to us, his loyal subjects. "I'm going to go on. I have a feeling that he is still out here, we would have seen him on our way out or he would have stopped us. He must be up this way somewhere."

"But, Sir—"

The Captain interjected, much to Hughes' annoyance, "No, I've made my mind up. I'm carrying on. I will find him, even if that means I only come back with a body. I owe it to him at the very least. You don't have to come with me, any of you."

He directed his gaze towards the Sergeant, who was clearly against continuing, but out of a blind loyalty to Captain Arnold, was going to go anyway.

"Well, we've come this far, Sir. We may as well carry on. Even if that is to stop you from going to ask the Germans where McKay's got to."

He gave a melancholy chuckle, that died out as quickly as his smile.

"Come on then, let's get a move on."

The silence was captivating and for a few, blissful seconds, I felt like a pebble on the shoreline, slowly being worn away of any jagged edges, any blemishes, leaving only a smoothed stone that felt soft to the touch.

In the same instant however, the stillness of the night began to chill my blood, as if I was already dead, the very tips of my fingers turning a shade of purple in the midnight air. It felt almost as though nature itself was conspiring against us, granting the enemy perfect listening conditions. All they would need to hear was a misplaced breath, carried through the stagnant air, or a slight rustle as a rock slipped beneath my feet.

I was feeling more vulnerable than I ever had done before.

While giving me both peace and fear, the silence too astounded me. It felt odd after what felt like months upon months of constant noise, there was now a perfect tranquillity in the air. I supposed that it was while either side caught their breath after what had happened; the Germans so that they could regroup and reorganise, the British so that they could keep a careful watch over the lunatics who had ventured out into the darkness once more.

Suddenly, our crawling human chain ground to a halt. I caught sight of Sergeant Hughes' arm as he beckoned us up closer to him and the Captain. Upon arriving there, we all stared at the same thing, wondering what it was doing and how it had got there.

A length of rope was coiled around the top of a shell hole, its one visible end beginning to fray, displaying its wonderful array of yarns and strands, all braided together to give it its extra strength. It was a chunky bit of rope, about two inches thick and so must have been a great burden to those who had carried them over to the frontline earlier on in the night.

It was definitely our bit of rope, there was no doubt about that. Above all else, it was cleaner than anything else in No Man's Land, its yellowing fibres only just taking on a slight pigment of damp brown on its underside, which meant that it hadn't been here very long at all.

The Captain was oblivious to anything else that went on around him now, he was focused entirely on the rope. Hughes took control, leaning back signalling to us to keep our eyes peeled and expect the worst.

We slid down, expecting to be met with the sight of a dead comrade. The crater was not as deep as it had looked from above, the water that sat at the bottom slowly beginning to dry out and become shallower. But it was still deep enough to give my feet an extra bathe.

The shell hole itself, apart from the water and its four new occupants, was completely empty of anything, other than the length of rope that drooped dimly into the water below.

I followed the journey of the rope, entering the crater from the British side of the opening and dipping down into the water, where it was inevitably still tied tightly around the waist. I knew the exact knot that was used, and where it actually fell on his hip as I had been the one to have tied it.

I recognised the German straight away, his blushed youthful cheeks still burning as brightly as they possibly could, while his nose was still bent at an ever so slightly odd angle. It was definitely him, he was our missing prisoner.

Captain Arnold scrambled his way over to him briefly, sliding the body upwards and out of the water for a quick inspection. Two substantial pits had been opened up on the young German's chest, close enough together for them to have both been from a quick double tap of the trigger, but far away enough to make two distinctive wounds. They had been fired from close range and, judging by the amount of blood and fleshy bits of tissue sprayed around the far side of the hole, they had passed right the way through his body. His insides would have been a total mess, as the bullets sucked more into their path as they travelled at a lightning speed.

He looked like he had been executed in cold blood.

We all had the same thought. It was Bob who spoke first, in defence of McKay.

"Maybe the German was dragging him back to the German frontline? So, he made sure he could make it back? Besides, he already knew we had the one prisoner that we would need."

We thought about it, wanting every word of it to be true.

"But he could have just cut him loose, surely," I uttered, "the German was unarmed. He was hardly going to shoot him in the back, was he?"

"And look at the size of McKay compared to this little lad. There's no way he would have been able to pull him more than a couple of yards, even if McKay only had one leg."

The Captain was frozen once again in his own moment of contemplation, struggling with the fact that one of his best soldiers had executed one of their hard-earned prisoners. He was just as puzzled as we all were.

"Sir?" breathed Hughes, "What do you reckon? Is it worth carrying on?"

"Yes," he said snapping out of his trance that were quite quickly becoming a dangerous habit. "I don't know what happened here, but McKay can't be too much further away from this hole, the body is still boiling hot. I would have expected it to cool down quickly out here. It's just a question of which way he would have gone."

He looked at us in turn as if we held the answer somehow, before the cogs began to whir in his mind over what to do next.

"The logical thing to do would be to turn straight back and make for the British lines, but he knew the Germans could have heard his gunshots. What I would do would be to deviate left or right, so that if a patrol came out it would be more difficult to trace him."

None of us had any thoughts, but silently agreed with him that it was perhaps the best course of action.

"Sergeant, you wait here. Try and keep an eye on us if you can. If we don't find him, we'll come back here and head in a straight line back to our trenches. How does that sound?"

I didn't like the idea of venturing out again, travelling adjacent to the German lines for an indeterminable amount of time. But, then again, I didn't much like the idea of staying in a shell hole on my own with a corpse. It seemed that all the straws were painfully short in this lot.

I wasn't sure how many more times I could follow Captain Arnold out into the unknown, but I quite quickly found myself doing it once again, in what felt like the hundredth time that night.

All I could do was clutch hold of my rifle tightly, until I could feel my knuckles turning white.

17

I COULD BARELY BRING myself to even breathe at the thought of how close we were to the German frontline. My apprehension was exaggerated by the faint tones of voices that wafted out and over the top of the parapet as we lay in the mud.

I wasn't expecting any kind of a counter attack or even a marksman taking pot-shots towards our lines tonight, as I imagined they would have been far more preoccupied with cleaning up the mess that we had left behind.

We had taken them by complete surprise and managed to dispatch of at least ten enemy soldiers during our short time in their dugout. If the other raids had had similar success, then there was a good chance that we had wiped out enough men to fill the ranks of an entire platoon, which would mean replacements would be needed to plug the gaps immediately.

The machine gun that was in one of the dugouts had also been destroyed, and I imagined a German quartermaster running around behind the lines, trying to source a spare one from wherever he could. Or maybe he was in the workshop right now, trying to patch it up again and make it serviceable.

The trenches themselves had taken a battering also, with the amount of explosives that we had managed to throw in causing more than a few sandbags to be ripped open in the blast. With any luck, we had done some serious structural damage to the trench, meaning that they would be more engrossed in fixing that, than the three figures that were crawling a mere stone's throw away from their lines.

We moved slowly, consistently, never moving a muscle which was out of step with the others. If there was a sentry on duty peering out over the moonless night, then he would be less likely to see a slow-moving object as he scanned the horizon.

Captain Arnold suddenly rolled over, as if he had grown tired of crawling around on his belly and was now opting to slither along on his back. But instead he disappeared, into another slight depression in the ground that would afford us a diminutive bit of cover.

I was completely breathless and, as we sat there clutching at our rifles, I realised that the fear that was harboured in my stomach had returned, manifesting as a faint quiver in my hands. I needed something to steady them, to calm myself down and I needed it fairly urgently. This was as good an opportunity as I was going to get, so I decided I would go for it.

As I reached for my breast pocket, my hands comforted by the solid feel of Sergeant Needs' hip flask, I ran through in my mind what I was going to say to the Captain when he saw me produce it.

"Sorry, Sir," I mumbled, ashamed at how it appeared

that I had disobeyed a direct order, "I couldn't leave without it. Would you like some?"

But the imaginary explanation never got that far. Before I could unbutton the pocket, there was movement on the other side of the slight ditch in the ground.

What had been, until very recently at least, a corpse suddenly burst into life, as it leapt from one side of the hole to the other.

Bob and I were both caught unawares, and we didn't have enough time to bury an entire complement of rounds into the body.

The Captain too had been caught with his guard down and before my brain had the time to register the movement, there was already a revolver being pressed down hard into the forehead of the Captain.

I felt like I had let the Captain down tremendously, he had led us with the most valiant of hearts and one of the most experienced minds. He had put faith in both Bob and me when we had proven ourselves no more than any of the other brand-new recruits that were flooding into France.

I had watched him command as a hero and now, I was forced to watch him die as one.

But then, the revolver eased, pulled away from the Captain's face and suddenly something altogether less threatening, as if the murderous silhouette had had a change of heart. The figure slumped back down on the other side of the divot, taking up the exact same patch of dirt that he had been in a few moments before.

There was a total silence for a moment, the void filled with a tension and humidity that hindered my breathing. I thought about bringing my weapon to bear and pumping a round or two into where I supposed the chest would be.

But, before I could, the Captain spoke. His voice was crackled and hoarse, and it seemed like, in amongst the desperation, that he had surrendered his aristocratic tones and for a moment sounded like one of the working-class lads that he commanded.

"McKay…"

I caught a glimpse of his face as he turned it away from us slightly and was relieved to recognise him. There was no need for me to pump this figure full of bullets.

His chiselled features; the square jaw and strong cheekbones that had appeared so unremarkable to me at first, became the finest face that I had ever laid eyes on. I was so pleased to see him.

As he whipped off the woollen hat that we all had pulled over our heads, his hair, like it was in a photograph came into view. He rubbed his hands through the greasy mess, as it seemed like he was rubbing even more colour out of it.

He looked at each of us in turn. His eyes were bloodshot and puffy and, had his face not been smothered with grease and charred cork, I was certain that I would have been able to see the great stains of tears that had rolled down his face. From where I was, it looked like he wasn't quite finished balling his eyes out just yet.

No one seemed like they knew quite what to do, it was a unique situation to say the least.

"McKay…What are you doing out here? What happened to your prisoner?" I could tell that Captain Arnold wanted to launch into a barrage of questions, asking far more and far less politely than he had done. But McKay had been fragile since we had met him, and he appeared even more so right now. He had to bide his time in searching for some answers, he just needed to coax him back to our lines for now.

Without warning, McKay burst into fits of tears once again, as if the only reason he had stopped was because of the interrupting figures who had slid towards him. His sobs were loud and sucking, and the Captain lurched for him as if he was going to cup his hand over his mouth. We had made it a long way without too many hiccups, we didn't want to fall at this hurdle now.

The Captain refrained from pressing his palm into McKay's mouth, instead opting to let the man speak, as he tried to form words in amongst the weeps and sighs.

"I was on my way back to the German lines, Captain… I left my satchel over there. I thought I would be able to get it back while they were all still in a confusion."

"Your satchel? What are you on about man, why's that important?"

"I thought if I was able to get it, then maybe none of it would matter so much. They had so many wounded and dead that there's a chance that they still haven't picked it up yet. I thought I could make amends, Sir.

"But there was too many bullets Captain Arnold. Honestly, I tried so hard, really, I did. I was just about to get back in and all the machine guns opened up. I was pinned down…"

Captain Arnold tried his best to comfort him as well as he could, McKay's distressed storytelling progressively getting louder as he bawled his eyes out. After a few more seconds, the Captain pressed him for more answers.

"And your prisoner, McKay. What happened to him? We found his body about thirty yards back that way."

"I was trying to keep him alive, I thought he would be

able to help me get back into the German lines. But when I realised that it wasn't going to work, I put some bullets in him. He was going to die anyway, no matter which way we ran. I killed him Sir…I killed him…"

"Alright, McKay, alright."

The Captain didn't seem to know what to do or say, as he looked over at both Bob and me with helpless little eyes. Instead, I offered him an option of what to do next.

GRHMN.

The hip flask was a welcome sight to the Captain, who looked at it warily for a moment before grasping it with full vigour. He took a sip himself, making his face screw up like a piece of paper, before passing it to McKay, who took an equally painful sip.

Captain Arnold passed it back to me, before pulling himself back into his commanding personality.

"Sargent keep an eye on what's going on around us would you. Don't want to end up dead after all this."

Bob rolled onto his stomach, bringing his rifle up and peered out towards the German lines. Captain Arnold was obviously still thinking of a job for me, as he turned back to McKay to question him further.

"I don't understand why you were going back McKay? I can't get my head around it. You weren't considering desertion, were you? Seeing out the rest of the war in some prisoner of war camp?"

McKay looked up, staring the Captain dead in the eyes with an expression as serious as a dead man's.

"What? No, Sir. Definitely not," he began to stare down at the ground with embarrassment. "Although probably something far worse than that, I'm afraid, Sir."

The Captain said nothing, just looked upon him with a

face that demanded to know everything, and soon.

"You know how I've been feeling the last few days, you're the only one I've really managed to tell. But after I got Dornan and Peterson killed, I wanted the war to be over. I felt even worse when Ellis and Sargent came in to replace them. It was awful for me to see their beds being used by two other blokes.

"I need the war to be over soon Sir, I don't think I can take much more of it. I'd be better off dead. I thought that if the Germans had some intelligence, something that they could use against us, then maybe this war would be over. One swift breakthrough here and then a flanking movement north and south, the war could be over in a couple of months.

"At the very least I was hoping that it could get us moved off this little patch. I needed somewhere new to carry on fighting, if I had to. I don't know what I was thinking, Sir…"

His weeping resurfaced, as I heard Bob shuffle around behind me with anticipation of the German patrol that would be sent out to investigate the noise. We could only hope that they were still struggling for men to plug the gaps in the line, never mind sending out a patrol.

"I stole some maps after the briefing Sir, from headquarters. It wasn't all that difficult, I said that you had requested them for tonight's raid. I put them in my satchel, along with the jam tins and rope that I had."

"So that's where you kept disappearing earlier on."

McKay nodded.

"But Sir, as soon as I left the Boche trench I regretted it immediately, I was on my way back to retrieve them. It's stupid I know, but I thought I'd be able to get them back before they realised what they were. I was hoping to use the prisoner as a bargaining chip if necessary. You have to believe me Sir, I was trying to make up for it, honest."

His sobs began to become more substantial, which immediately concerned the Captain.

"It's alright, McKay. We can talk this through. But we're probably going to have to move, we need to try and get you back behind our lines. We'll talk properly then."

I couldn't tell if it was a genuine sympathy that Captain Arnold was displaying, or a survival instinct that was working in overdrive to keep all of us alive. Compassionately, he put his arm around McKay's shoulder.

He obviously hadn't listened to what Captain Arnold had been saying to him, as he soon burst into another torrent of apologies and justifications for what he had done. Captain Arnold tried to stifle his hysteria by holding him closer into his own body, but nothing seemed to work.

"I was about to shoot myself Sir when you three fell into this ditch. Honestly, I didn't know what I was thinking."

McKay was a broken man. He had clearly seen and done things that no one could ever imagine, and now they were beginning to exploit the cracks that had begun to appear in his mind. It struck me as odd, yet rather humbling, that a man like him; built like a coastal defence boulder, could have such a fragile mind. But I supposed that was what this war was doing to men all across the continent.

"I'm sorry, Sir. Truly I am."

"It's okay McKay. Ellis, pass me that hip flask again."

Bob's feet scuffled behind me as I moved.

"Shh," he rasped urgently. "Someone's coming."

18

I could just about make out a faint crunching noise as an indeterminable number of boots made contact with the ground around them. The soft scrunching noise gradually grew louder, until it became slightly distorted by the damp mud that they were stepping into.

I tried to count the pairs of feet as they walked, but quite quickly had to give up, I had more important things to do.

I forced my rifle away from my chest and checked to see if it was all ready to go. It had to be, I'd checked numerous times already. I just had to pray that the young lad who had, until very recently, owned this rifle, had paid as much attention to it as I did my own.

I would also have to hope that rolling around in this mud and dirt hadn't got anything into the internals where it shouldn't have been. I particularly hoped that the young owner hadn't put the full complement of ten rounds in the breech because, if he had, there was an increased chance of two rounds getting in the way of each other when I pulled the trigger. Enhanced even more by the fact that I had shaken this rifle round more than a door knocker.

My mind was awash with the negatives of the situation, plagued by all the possibilities of what might go wrong. If the gun jammed, it jammed, I knew how to clear it and I also knew that I could rely on at least two of my comrades to be up and firing if the situation demanded it. I was still hoping that it wouldn't come to that.

As the footsteps became more audible, I was surprised at the obvious lack of voices amongst whoever it was that was making their way towards us. I assumed that there was more than one of them, as it would have been complete suicide to come out here alone.

When we had moved, there had been the odd command, the occasional whisper, but whoever the feet belonged to moved in a complete silence, a ghostlike absence of noise.

My first instinct was that it was Sergeant Two Pews, making his way back over to us after seeing that we had been immobile for some time. I thought that it might add a humour to the situation if he was to suddenly pop his head over the side of the ditch, peer in and see each of us quivering next to our rifles as we felt like we'd been stalked.

But I could tell by Bob's face, who had now slithered down to meet us at the bottom of the ditch, that the figure or figures that he had seen, were not the ones that belonged to the Sergeant, but to someone completely unknown to him.

Things were beginning to look pretty bleak.

Then, as if nature broke its conspiracy against us, there was a slight breeze, that floated over the top of the ditch.

The breeze in itself did nothing to calm me, but it was what it carried along that was of interest to us all.

There was a whisper. A slight recognition of a voice. Which meant there was more than one hunter out to get us.

It was only a short sound, maybe one word or command, but it was enough to distinguish it as foreign to the English language.

It was guttural and harsh, almost as if it had been invented so that one person could spit at another, or to constantly clear their throats.

I looked across at McKay, who had perked up slightly since the crisis had begun, who mouthed one word at me, quite clearly.

German.

I wondered if he could hear what they were saying, if he could understand what was going on and considered for a moment moving myself, so that I could sit next to him and gain the upper hand in hiding from the patrol. But the noise I would generate would render that advantage null and void, and so I opted to cower where I was, until I was forced to move.

We could do nothing, apart from stare at one another's blackened faces and swallow hard. I tried to focus on my breathing, making sure that my breaths were slow and deliberate, not making too much noise but equally not short changing myself. All I could feel like doing was wheezing and sighing as loud as I wanted to.

I distracted myself by looking at the other faces in the shallow ditch that could quite soon become my grave.

Bob was staring at me with a wild stare, like he had suddenly become obsessed with me and everything that I was doing. I wanted to get him to shut them, as they glared so brightly it was like being out in the middle of a full moon. But instead all I could do was emulate the fear that was scratched into his eyeballs.

Captain Arnold sat quite patiently, as if he had been here a thousand times before and knew exactly how it would end. I wished that I had the same confidence as he did, but the quiver in my hands was back, and I could do nothing to reassure myself in the same way the Captain was.

McKay surprisingly looked quite at peace. He had a look on his charred face that was one of resignation, as if he had concluded ages ago that he would die tonight, and every second that he stayed alive was some sort of a bonus. I supposed for a man that was about to blow his own mind out not two minutes before, that this was some kind of a stay of execution of sorts.

I dreaded to think what my own face conveyed to my comrades. I wasn't scared of being afraid, but I was petrified of the others thinking me a coward, especially when my hands were shaking like a wet dog. My every instinct told me to reach for the hip flask, but I tried to override my own desires, a thick coating of sweat dripping down from every possible pore in my body. I was a mess.

To become more of an effective soldier, I decided to ponder the reasons for a German patrol at this time of night, as if that would give me some sort of an edge as to what kind of weapons they might be carrying, or how fast they would be wanting to move.

My mind went through all manner of possibilities. They could have been a patrol that had quickly been rustled together, in response to seeing a group of British soldiers leap out from their lines again. Or maybe they had even seen McKay and his prisoner stumbling about in No Man's Land and they were out to find them.

In which case there was a chance that they were very lightly armed on account of the spontaneity of the operation. But there was also a possibility that they had managed to dispatch of Sergeant Hughes and would be incensed at the discovery of their friends' corpse. I was sure they would be in no mood for mercy or compassion.

It was probably more likely that they were a wiring party, out to fix the coils of wire that we had snapped to allow for an easier approach. That would surely be one of their priorities right now. But we were further away from our entry point here. Maybe they were lost. Or maybe they had more than one sector to fix. But it was quite possible that they weren't a rewiring party at all.

I had heard stories in the last few days of a mythical marksman in the German army, who ventured out into No Man's Land in the middle of the night, with a few of his cronies. He would set up camp somewhere with good vision, camouflaging himself as well as he could do in the darkness. Then, by morning, he was in prime position to begin picking off the British frontline soldiers at the faintest whiff of a skull.

It was true that more and more men had been getting dropped in the last week or so, which would explain the spectral sharpshooter theory. Perhaps we had stumbled into his hideout and that soon, we would come face to face with the murderer himself, who would no doubt have no hesitations in butchering us all.

The noises were growing louder and louder, not enough to alert the British frontline troops, but enough to make us feel like the countdown clock was suddenly ticking a lot faster than it had been previously.

As I began to move my finger towards the trigger, anxious to take control of my own situation and bury these soldiers in the ground, the Captain began to shuffle around, unnecessarily garishly. He was rummaging around in his satchel, the one that had housed the maps and papers that we had stolen from the Germans.

I wondered if perhaps he was going to use them, to bargain for our lives with, as I hadn't seen him hand them over to anyone when we had re-entered our own lines. But surely Arnold would have been more aware than to travel back out with the stolen intelligence in tow. But I couldn't think of any other reason for his fumbling.

I was transfixed by what he was doing, and it wasn't as if I could really look anywhere else. I could feel the other two pairs of eyes, burning holes in the side of the Captain's face as he struggled to free whatever it was he was trying to withdraw.

Suddenly, I thought about Sergeant Hughes, and wondered if he knew how close to death we really were, or if he was unaware of our peril. There was a chance that he might have simply returned to our lines immediately. I still wasn't quite sure what kind of a man he was.

After what felt like an eternity, Arnold's wrist suddenly reappeared from the top of the bag, followed by his hands which were clamped tightly around something.

The Very Pistol.

He withdrew it completely and adjusted it so that it sat perfectly in his hand. I wondered what he was intending to do with it, but I fairly quickly got my answer.

I glared at him, as if to scream 'No!', but he was none

the wiser. He was in his own little world right now. All I could do was exactly what the other two were doing; watch him, trust him and pray that he had thought everything through properly. If he hadn't done that last bit, then we could expect a whole heap of trouble to come down on our heads at any moment, literally.

His face was completely deadpan, but I could tell that he was enjoying this. He enjoyed having a hold over all of us, each of his subjects completely helpless to his whims and impulses. He was still quite calm, not experiencing the kind of hand tremors that were still shaking their way up my arm. It felt as if my brain was being shaken in the same way.

I watched with horror and a hint of admiration as he pulled the pistol upright, angling up and towards the night sky. I looked up expectantly, waiting for the moment where the inky blackness suddenly became filled with a brilliant white light, like a heavenly host had descended to bring us good news.

Except the only news I was expecting was piercing hot lead as it seared my flesh.

The scraping as the figures got closer and closer to us grew even louder, and I could tell that they were pretty much on top of us. They had stopped whispering to one another now and, even if they hadn't then I wouldn't have cared too much.

We knew where they were, and they seemed confident that they didn't need to hide their presence.

I readied myself for what could be my final few seconds, as I wondered why Captain Arnold was taking so long in depressing the trigger. It felt like I was staring down the barrels of my firing squad, the Captain making them hold their fire for just half a second more.

He raised the pistol up ever so slightly, so it was roughly chest height, but far enough away from his face that his nose wasn't going to go up with the flare.

Then, looking down at us for half a second, he grinned.

I was certain that I made out the top of one the German's heads as he waddled his way ever closer to us. But I couldn't quite get a good enough look. As I turned, Captain Arnold squeezed the trigger and the flare rose high into the sky.

I was blinded.

19

THE FLARE INITIATED the now familiar dancing shadows, as everything basked in its artificial light for a few seconds. It wiggled as it slowly began its descent to earth, every inanimate object suddenly becoming alive while the live ones all stood stock still.

It hissed and cracked as I wondered what would happen next. For a moment or two, nothing did. We all just sat and watched the flare continue to carve its own path to the ground.

I enjoyed watching it for a moment, my burning eyes momentarily at the back of my mind as I marvelled at the way such a small contraption could generate so much light. It felt like I was a child again, the one who was petrified by the dark but, come morning was celebrating in the light that daybreak brought with it.

The German's shadows moved far more than they did themselves, long, grotesque phantoms of darkness stretched out over the top of us, reaching out to the far side of our little ditch.

I could make out at least four individual shadows, each one of them appearing to belong to a human counterpart, but that wasn't to say that they were the only ones out here, in fact, there could be as many as ten or fifteen, especially if they were trying to mount a retaliatory raid on our line.

The figures that towered above us were just half a second too late in hitting the ground. The boys back in our frontline were alert, the Captain had told them to be so, and it had paid off.

All of a sudden, an eruption ensued, as if a horizontal volcano was spewing molten lava in every direction. I could see no rounds from where I was, but I could hear them being spat from the guns and then their impacts in the dirt all around the ditch that I was camped in. For once, I felt something that reminded me of being safe.

Every gun that was within range seemed to open up, sidearms included, as a great barrage of murderous projectiles found their targets and sent bits of blood and flesh flying in every direction, a warm rain falling on our heads for a second or two.

A pang of sadness suddenly twanged from somewhere deep within me for the Germans. They had unsuspectingly found themselves lit up like a Christmas tree and had no more than half a second to react before our boys were pumping them full of bullets.

We could have waited, to see if they had passed us and headed back to their own lines, but instead, we had signed their death warrant. I could hear the sick ripping of flesh as limbs were torn from their sockets, both partially and completely, their soft groans of agony quickly interrupted by another burst of bullets to their body.

The resounding noise was one of sobering thuds, as body after body collapsed into an untidy heap on the floor, whereupon they still took rounds to their being, even after all the air had left their lungs.

Suddenly, there was a great ruckus as a body careered into the ditch, as if he was trying to do his best impression of a flying squirrel. His rifle went flying off in the opposite direction to him and landed neatly beside the Captain.

He instantly began scrabbling around trying to find it, to see if he could return a meagre amount of fire in memoriam of his dead comrades.

He noticed the four bodies that were sat around the ditch, all now glaring at him intently. He was obviously having the same struggles that we had had when we first slid into the ditch; trying to make the distinction as to whether the bodies he was looking at were dead or alive.

The figure must have noticed the difference quite quickly, consequently setting about the task to identify whether they were friendly or enemy faces that he was staring at.

The rattle of machinegun fire, interspersed with the never-ending backdrop of rifle cracks, continued incessantly above our heads, the rounds still meeting their marks with impressive precision. There was no way that he was going to want to risk scrabbling back out there, even if there was less than a second left from the flare.

Just before the flare began to fizzle out, it was clear that the German soldier had made up his mind about what he was about to do. He was going to die, so he might as well take at least one of us with him.

With a low, fearsome growl, the figure sprang from his resting place, fixing his eyes on the first person that he saw and the one that he suddenly became determined to kill. From the moment that he made his first movements, it was clear to see that Bob was his intended target, but he was just a little too slow in reacting, and so he allowed the German to crash into him with the ferocity and speed of an express train.

The German, with no rifle to hand, had no visible weapons that I could see, but it made the situation no less perilous for Bob, who now had a pair of rough, thick hands clamped tightly around his wind pipe.

The machineguns raging above us just about drowned out all of the noise that was coming from the two fighting figures, but I could make out, every now and then, the rasps of Bob as he struggled for air.

He managed to bring a fist up and connect it well with the side of the German's head, but it simply wasn't enough to throw him off. Bob was growing weaker by the second, the German seemingly growing more powerful.

He continued to throw wild punches around, each one growing increasingly weaker as his body couldn't keep up with the demands of the situation. His legs bucked and kicked, aiming for the groin, but nothing would throw the German off from taking one last victim with him to the grave.

We were dumbfounded for a moment, in disbelief that against such overwhelming odds, the German still fought for his Kaiser. None of us jumped in to help Bob instinctively, but we grabbed our rifles all the same, wistfully hoping more than anything that an opportunity would present itself to take the shot.

The confines were too cramped though, and the tussle suddenly took a turn in Bob's favour as, in what well could have been a last-ditch attempt at survival, he flipped the German onto his back and pounced upon him like a ravenous lion.

There was no way we could take the shot safely, we didn't know if the German would suddenly gain the upper hand, and the bullet we had just aimed at his head would find its way into Bob's stomach. That was without taking into consideration the number of survivors above us; if they heard a rifle crack, then there was a possibility that we could have a platoon of hard-nosed, battle-ready Germans falling on our heads. And enough had already gone wrong tonight.

The grunts and grimaces continued for half a second more before a fist the size of a football slammed down hard on top of Bob's skull. He crumpled on top of the German, who quickly found the energy to roll Bob off him and take the upper hand once more, but it would be the last thing he would do.

McKay lunged at him, bayonet drawn and firmly in his grasp. If there had been more light I was certain his knuckles would have been white with intensity.

McKay was controlled, calm almost, as he stopped just short of the tussle and slid the bayonet expertly into the man's neck, continuing to push from right to left until I thought the bayonet would appear out of the other side. He drove it in firmly, but almost like he was trying to do it without causing too much pain to the man, which he must have achieved, as the man lay silent as he withdrew the offending weapon.

It was all over faster than if a bullet had shot from one side to the next, and I could make out great bloody tears running over both McKay's and Bob's faces as they sucked in the fresher air of freedom for a moment or two.

McKay rolled the body off Bob's chest, affording him some freedom to begin recovering and profusely thanking McKay for saving his life. McKay ignored him, instead opting to wipe his bayonet on the back of the German's tunic and retreat to where he had been sat previously.

As he did so, the Captain, making sure to keep his head nice and low, crawled his way over to the corpse of the German, verifying his death and checking for any additional intelligence that he could present to his superiors.

"Thank you…Thank you," repeated Bob over and over, in an exaggerated whisper that was either down to the throttling he had just received, or out of an awareness that there could still be more just inches above our heads.

The flare suddenly went out, plunging us once again into the familiar darkness that we had been waiting for. Now, we would be able to move. Hopefully, within the next hour, I would be back in our lines and on our way to the *Café de Fleurs,* but anything could happen out here.

McKay began to sob uncontrollably. The water burst forth as if a dam had suddenly given way, the oncoming stream obliterating everything within its wake. His chin trembled awfully, and I watched as the muscles in his face went into overdrive as they fought against the cries, and tried to bring his face back into order.

He seemed like a child for a while, the crying so raw and unblemished that it was as if the pain that was coursing through his body was a physical one, a wound somewhere having opened up and causing an incredible weeping. His hands were tightly clamped into defiant fists, as if he knew he needed to stop, but fighting the urge was futile.

"McKay...McKay...it's okay. We're going back now. Relax."

I couldn't think of any other words to utter into his ear as I pressed him into my chest, so I repeated them over and over again as he slowly began to calm himself down, the sobs soon turning into nothing other than desperate gasps for air.

He was more like a child than ever before, softly breathing within my embrace, as I soothingly repeated the words to him, trying to bring him back to reality.

His breathing and general behaviours suddenly became erratic once more, as a burst of gunfire suddenly rattled over our heads, a mixture of the booming machineguns and solitary cracks of rifle fire.

McKay buried his head into my chest, as I tucked my head over the top of his, pressing it in so firmly that I thought he might begin to burrow through at any second. I bit down hard on the backs of my teeth as I grimaced my way through the latest attempt to sever my mental from my physical being.

I couldn't for the life of me work out why they were firing, especially as there was no source of illumination to speak of now, and consequently no real chance of hitting whatever it was they thought they were aiming at.

Maybe they were making sure that their men were dead, so that they couldn't be picked up and patched up by our troops as additional prisoners. It was unlikely, but not an impossibility.

The chances were that they were merely doing it to

make themselves feel a bit better. You're more likely to hit a target if you pull the trigger, than if you don't.

The sweeping gunfire continued for a few minutes more, and I clamped my eyes shut on more than one occasion, when the whines of bullets passing overhead resounded far more often than I perhaps would have liked.

There was nothing that we could do, except wait it out, alone with our own thoughts and the other silent silhouettes who were perched beside us.

I was trying my best to protect McKay from the noise, as if that would somehow restore his confidence and sanity, but I was struggling to come across as reassuring as I would have liked. My hands had started to tremble, and an almighty headache had begun to burn at the front of my head. I put it down to the incredible noise of the last few minutes, coupled with the burningly bright light, that had seared my eyes to the point that I thought I would go blind.

I reached for the hip flask. It was the only thing that seemed like it could give me some sort of relief.

20

A SERENE SILENCE suddenly stretched across the entire landscape. Nothing seemed to move for entire minutes, a phenomenon that I had not experienced for what felt like an eternity. It had been so long since I had experienced silence, and the accompanying lack of movement of anything around me, that I quite quickly felt uneasy, scared almost.

Surely something will give in a second.

I waited and waited, alone with my thoughts as I gradually convinced myself that out of the silence, death would sneak up on me.

Any moment now. Any second and I will be dead.

I held my breath for what felt like five minutes but wasn't anything more than two or three seconds. Everyone else did the same, including the dead Germans.

But still, as we strained our ears to the point of bleeding, there was no noise, not even any rustling about in the German frontline just a matter of yards away.

We waited for a few minutes more, just to ensure that

we weren't going to be lit up the moment we peered over the top of the shallow ditch.

My uniform was soaked through, a mixture of sweat and dirty rainwater, and it clung to me like a second skin. I couldn't wait to shed it the minute we got back to the café. I quickly rebuked myself.

Too much hope, Andrew. It'll get you killed.

I couldn't lose sight of Sergeant Needs' advice now, I had come through a lot this evening on the back of it.

The night, from our point of view, had largely been one of catastrophe and close calls. I felt particularly despondent at the initial wave of pride and success that I had felt when we had first left the German frontline.

But now, my pride was well and truly dented, beyond recognition, and I gave myself a stern talking to that, if I was to see through tonight, then I would never feel pleased or proud of what I had done until my war was over; whether that meant the end of the war itself, or when I was staring at the underside of a coffin lid.

I wondered for a moment what was going to happen to us. Would we face some sort of disciplinary action for venturing back out into No Man's Land? Or would it be medals for our bravery?

I couldn't get the thought to leave my mind for another few minutes before I looked over at the Captain, and stared at his apprehensive face.

He was a fantastic leader, one who had been willing to sacrifice himself, as well as the rest of his other men, for one man who had lost his way for a few, pivotal moments. But now, he had put us all in danger for McKay, he had gone against orders and ignored the signs of a weakening soldier.

None of this would have happened if he had stuck by protocol and it certainly wouldn't have happened if McKay had been removed from the team.

Ultimately, the buck stopped with Captain Arnold, the one who was in charge of each of us and the strain was showing on his face mightily. He was in his own little world again, the one that he seemed so comfortable and peaceful in, but this time he was concerned.

He abruptly caught my eye for a moment before he pulled himself from his stupor and back into officer mode.

He rolled over onto his stomach, sliding his rifle up beside him as if he was giving it the chance to look over the lip of the hole with him. He allowed the tops of his eyes to just rise up over the edge of the hole, but stopped quickly, not wanting to put any more flesh on display than was strictly necessary.

Arnold signalled for us all to bow in towards him as he spoke, so that his voice wasn't carried along by the swarming silence.

"I reckon it's about time we went back now, what do you reckon? Out of here, across No Man's Land and back to our lines. All quite simple really."

I couldn't wait to get back, I was practically shaking at the prospect of finally being relatively safe again. The tremble in my fingertips had worsened, and I craved the fear and excitement that I so clearly needed to steady them again.

The one other thing that I had found myself craving was some of Earnshaw's paraffin. It was stronger than the stuff that Needs had had, but it had tasted so much sweeter than anything else before.

I had necked so much of the stuff in that little ditch, as

had the Captain and the others, that I was soon shaking around a near-empty hip flask that had no more than a few solitary drops clinging to the inside of its chamber.

As I sat there, rotating it in my palms for something to distract from the trembling, I realised it wasn't so much a craving anymore, but a need. It was slowly giving me the confidence to do things in this war that I never thought imaginable before I discovered it. It was what had made me leave the trenches for that very first advance and every act of bravery since.

It was beginning to take a hold on me, as if I felt like I needed it with me to operate effectively. I didn't feel like it was hindering my performance at all, and so felt no desires whatsoever to curtail my consumption of the stuff. There and then, I decided I would stock up on some of Earnshaw's supplies, just in case he snuffed it before I could replenish my barren flask. He'd already come close tonight.

"Let's get one thing clear though, before we make tracks. This," he pointed to the hole that we were perched in, "is to be our little secret. No one else is to know about what has happened tonight. No one outside our section. Understood?"

I nodded enthusiastically, as did Bob. McKay sat unresponsive, but attentive enough to know that he was taking it all in.

"If anyone let's slip, then that's it. McKay here will most likely be court martialled and shot. By association, you could hope for a prison sentence too. Your reputation will be shredded, your families ashamed of you. I'm not trying to scare you into staying silent, I'm being realistic."

He looked at us in turn, with a glare so stern that it was

clear that he would happily be a part of the firing squad himself, if he was to find out we'd said something.

"It could have happened to any one of us. We're all human, we're all vulnerable. Fear is a part of war. Understood?"

I waited for a few moments before saying anything, but when I did, I feared immediately that I had made some sort of mistake.

"Sir, the Germans will find the satchel eventually, their command will have it soon. How are we going to warn our boys that an attack could be coming, without telling them what's happened?"

He gave it some thought for a moment, heading into his own thoughts while staring at me unceasingly, as if he was annoyed that I had created some more mental work for him to do.

"I suppose I'll have to come up with something for them...I'll just tell them that there was a higher number of troops in their lines than what we had previously seen. Lead them into thinking that they're getting ready for an advance. Hopefully that way they'll make preparations for attacks in this sector."

I nodded obediently, as if he had commanded me to, but deep down I was conflicted as to whether or not the ploy would work. But I couldn't see any other way out of the predicament we had found ourselves in. This was our only way.

"Maybe it'll even work in our favour, launch a preemptive strike which captures the line. Who knows. Maybe this *will* help shorten the war after all, eh McKay?"

He looked over at him and gave him a smile, which was reciprocated only by a lengthy stare. The Captain was good to McKay, to the point where it felt almost like a fatherly bond existed between them, the Captain never able to stay angry at his son for too long, before the love for him shone through as he remedied all the issues.

It should have worried me, that the Captain was unable to let go of his men, but instead it comforted me, to know that everyone in this section would have one another's backs, and would willingly volunteer to crawl out into No Man's Land to find my corpse.

"Whatever happens, we must stick together as a section. Got it? No one goes awry."

I looked across at Bob in what felt like the first time in forever, comforted to see his blackened face and his turbulent little eyes staring straight back at me.

We'll be back soon enough, that's what he had shouted at our old platoon as we left to join Captain Arnold's team. But somehow, without speaking, we both knew that would never be the case now.

I wondered if he had ever believed in what he had said, or if he had known that we would never be going back there, as I had thought at the time. Maybe it had just been a flippant comment that he hadn't believed himself, or maybe he held a genuine belief that he would soon be back to a standard infantry soldier.

Whatever he believed, we were now bound to this section for the rest of our days, we were glued to one another by secrecy.

"Right then, chaps. Shall we try and make it back without any more dramas?"

As we began to roll around in the dirt, trying to make our way back to our lines, I realised something about the section that I was now obliged to serve for the rest of my life.

I enjoyed being here, I loved the excitement of what we were doing and there were no other men that I would want to be fighting with, than the ones that I had beside me in the section.

For me, I was no longer a soldier watching the likes of Arnold, Hughes, Earnshaw and McKay, but something different.

Now, I felt like one of the trench raiders.

THE END
Follow Sergeant Andrew Ellis and the team in the third book of the series, 'Invisible Frontline' - available to order on Amazon now!

YOU CAN HELP MAKE A DIFFERENCE

Reviews are one of my most powerful weapons in generating attention for my books.
Unfortunately, I do not have a blockbuster budget when it comes to advertising but
Thanks to you I have something better than that.

Honest reviews of my books helps to grab the attention of other readers so, even if you have one minute, I would be incredibly grateful if you could leave me a review on whichever Amazon store suits you.

THANK YOU SO MUCH.

GET A FREE BOOK TODAY

If you enjoyed this book, why not pick up another one, completely free?

'Enemy Held Territory' follows Special Operations Executive Agent, Maurice Dumont as he inspects the defences at the bridges at Ranville and Benouville. Fast paced and exciting, this Second World War thriller is one you won't want to miss!

Simply go to:

www.ThomasWoodBooks.com/free-book
To sign up!

ABOUT THE AUTHOR

Thomas Wood is the author of the 'Gliders over Normandy' series, The Trench Raiders, as well as the upcoming series surrounding Lieutenant Alfie Lewis, a young Royal Tank Regiment officer in 1940s France.

He posts regular updates on his website
www.ThomasWoodBooks.com

and is also contactable by email at
ThomasWoodBooks@outlook.com

twitter.com/thomaswoodbooks
facebook.com/thomaswoodbooks

Printed in Great Britain
by Amazon